"FOR G... THIS IS 1870!"

There was disgust in Jeff's voice. "Duels have been outlawed. Gentlemen don't solve their problems with a gun. When are you going to let go of this ridiculous theory of yours?"

"It's not ridiculous. It happened!"

"Well, you don't have to worry. I'm not going to shoot Sam Calvert."

A rush of shame went through Amelia. "I never thought you would shoot in cold blood. It's just that sometimes, circumstances—"

"No circumstances," Jeff replied with vehemence, "will ever persuade me to take up a gun against another man again. Do you understand, Amelia?" He turned eyes on her that were dark with a pain deeper than her accusations.

Jeff was innocent. Amelia knew that in her very soul. Her wits and her knowledge of what would happen were Jeff's only hope. And even if he ended up hating her, she had to find the answer that would save his future.

REBECCA FLANDERS

Rebecca Flanders published her first book in 1982. Since then, she has written more than fifty novels and enjoyed success in historical, romance, suspense, women's fiction, western adventure, women-in-jeopardy and time-travel genres. At Harlequin, Rebecca Flanders has written for Harlequin American Romance, Intrigue, Superromance, Harlequin Romance and Harlequin Presents, and is the author of the popular Dreamscape romance, *Earthbound*.

This prolific and popular author is a five-time finalist for the Golden Medallion Award for Excellence presented by Romance Writers of America, the recipient of two Lifetime Achievement awards and one Editor's Choice Award from *Romantic Times,* and a winner of the prestigious MAGGIE Award from Georgia Romance Writers.

Rebecca lives on the side of a mountain in North Georgia with a collie, a golden retriever and three cats. In her spare time she enjoys painting and long mountain hikes.

Watch for Rebecca Flanders's next title, *Once Upon A Time,* Harlequin American Romance #454, a September 1992 release.

REBECCA FLANDERS

Yesterday Comes Tomorrow

Harlequin Books

TORONTO • NEW YORK • LONDON
AMSTERDAM • PARIS • SYDNEY • HAMBURG
STOCKHOLM • ATHENS • TOKYO • MILAN
MADRID • WARSAW • BUDAPEST • AUCKLAND

YESTERDAY COMES TOMORROW

July 1992

ISBN 0-373-83247-8

Yesterday Comes Tomorrow

ONE

"Okay. It says here that Aury Island was first settled in 1640 by the Spanish, who found it inhabited by friendly natives...." Amelia Langston pushed at her sunglasses, which had slipped farther down on her nose with each dip the car took on the narrow, winding road. She glanced over at her friend, Peggy. "Why, do you suppose, if the natives were so friendly, the settlers always ended up having wars with them?"

Peggy Brewer took a hand off the steering wheel long enough to wave dismissively. "Forget the Spanish. Get to the good part."

Amelia returned to the brochure in her hand—one of several that had been sent to them courtesy of Aury Island Plantation in preparation for this weekend. She had been reading them off and on for most of the trip, partly to avoid becoming carsick, partly out of boredom, and partly as a way—although so far vainly—to generate some personal enthusiasm for the weekend ahead.

"'A thriving rice plantation that employed native islanders and Haitians, Aury Island was neutral during the Civil War...'"

"No, no, no. After that."

"'...and remained under the sole ownership of the Craig family until 1920,'" continued Amelia, disregarding Peggy. "'At that time, declining family fortunes forced the Craigs to abandon their ancestral home and sell off portions of the island to wealthy industrialists who built lavish homes on the north side of the island. In 1960, the majority of the island was purchased by an investment group that developed it into a luxurious family resort. However, the plantation house and its surrounding acreage is once again privately owned and has been restored to its former glory as both a working plantation and a luxury hotel. Antique furnishings and attention to period detail will enhance your stay at Aury Island Plantation. Waken to the sound of birds singing and the smell of breakfast being prepared on a wood-burning stove. Enjoy the view from the gallery of each of our twelve richly appointed rooms while sipping coffee or tea from Wedgwood china. Plan a day of horseback riding, hiking through our many wooded trails or take a trip back in time on one of our plantation tours. Whatever you choose, we're certain you will find Aury Island Plantation the perfect getaway and we look forward to welcoming you back, year after year.'"

With a sigh, Amelia looked around at the thick-leaved green foliage that brushed against the windows of the car and stretched ahead on both sides of the asphalt road as far as she could see. She said, with a hint of wistfulness in her voice, "Are you *sure* you wouldn't rather stay at one of those beachfront resort hotels?"

"For two hundred dollars a night? I'm game if you are. Your credit card or mine?"

"Well," admitted Amelia, "when you compare two hundred dollars a night for a beachfront room—"

"Plus meals and tips," Peggy reminded her.

"—to a complimentary weekend at the plantation playing mystery games with people we don't know—"

"Naturally, you take the free weekend."

"I'd take the beachfront room in a minute if I had two hundred dollars a night," Amelia said wryly.

"Come on, Amy, this is going to be fun!" Peggy pushed a button that lowered the power windows, and humid air rushed in. "Smell that air, will you? This place is a wildlife preserve. Did you know that? And all these tropical plants and great oaks—they're originals!"

"As opposed to imitations?" Amelia grimaced as she unsuccessfully tried to push back the wisps of frizzy hair stirred by the wind. Peggy, with her curly blond ponytail neatly protected by a colorful sun visor, was oblivious to the breeze, but Amelia's thick hair had begun to frizz the moment they crossed the South Carolina border, and no matter how tightly she coiled her hair away from her face she couldn't seem to keep it under control. "Please, the air conditioner?"

With an amused look, Peggy raised the windows again.

"Anyway," Amelia said, shifting in her seat, "it looks spooky, if you ask me." She gazed out the windshield at the huge twisted oaks and cypresses draped with gray moss, the dense bushes and twisted vines that grew in junglelike profusion. The heavy growth shadowed the road and created a close, almost-suffocating atmosphere, as though nature resented the intrusion of the outside world and was determined to resist its every encroachment. "Like things are crawling around in all that green stuff."

"What kinds of things?"

"Snakes and alligators and bugs." Amelia shuddered.

Peggy laughed. "What a wimp you are! Did you come wrapped in plastic, or what?"

"All I know is that there are no snakes on the beach."

"Unless you want to count the two-legged kind, of course. Oh, come on, Amy, look around you." Peggy made a wide gesture to include the passing greenery. "This is beautiful. It's nature, it's *history*. Where's your sense of romance?"

Peggy winced and apologetically looked over at Amelia. "Sorry, poor choice of words. What I meant was..." But she faltered.

Amelia smiled, though it felt a little forced. "For heaven's sake, Peggy, you don't have to tiptoe around me. I'm completely over what's his name."

She had been telling herself that every day for the past six weeks and still expected that one day she would say it and it would somehow, magically, be true. After all, she had only been with Bob for two years. She was twenty-nine years old, and two years was less than a tenth of her life. But two years of seeing the same face day after day, of working with him, dining with him, laughing with him and fighting with him— of learning his habits and peculiarities and letting him creep into every corner of her life... Amelia had a feeling it would take more than six weeks to get over him.

It wasn't as if she still loved Bob. Their love died long before the relationship had. It was simply that he had become so familiar, like a habit she didn't quite know how to break. Amelia didn't adjust well to change, and now she found herself facing two monumental changes—the loss of a lover and the loss of her job.

Bob had been the managing editor of a Richmond magazine for which she wrote a monthly food-and-nutrition column. Wandering into a relationship with him had seemed the most natural thing in the world—almost unavoidable. Now she knew the wisdom of the old adage that warned a woman never to date her boss. Although Bob had insisted they could maintain a professional relationship, Amelia disagreed. A clean break was the only kind of break she knew how to make, and even *that* wasn't as easy as she had expected.

When the invitation had come from Aury Island Plantation to join select members of the travel and entertainment industry in a complimentary mystery weekend to celebrate the opening of the restored plantation house as a luxury hotel, Amelia's first instinct had been to ignore it. Since she was no longer employed by Richmond's *Lifestyles,* she saw no point in reviewing restaurants for her own pleasure. Peggy, who owned a travel agency, had also received an invitation, and she'd badgered Amelia into accompanying her. Amelia could write an article, Peggy insisted, and use it to get another magazine job. And even if she didn't *want* another magazine job, she couldn't afford to ignore the contacts she might make at a place like this. Besides, it was free, and Amelia could definitely use a change of scenery. In the end Amelia had agreed because it was easier than resisting.

And the truth was, she would have enjoyed a vacation—at a nice, quiet beach hotel with towel boys and *mai tai*s, but not in some garish antebellum inn chasing down clues to a murder mystery.

She asked, "Couldn't we at least drive by and look at the beach?"

Peggy turned her wrist to look at the Art Deco watch there. "Well, okay. We have another hour to check in. Which way?"

Amelia quickly unfolded the brochure that included a map of the island. "Turn left on Nightingale Road. That should bring you right up behind the Seagrass Inn."

"I guess it wouldn't hurt to know where the nightlife is," Peggy conceded, making the turn. "In case we get bored."

"You can have the nightlife. I'm more interested in finding out where the good restaurants are. Who knows what kind of food they'll be serving at this place."

"With some of the top food critics in the Southeast coming—including yourself—you can bet they'll only be serving the best."

Amelia snorted. "Well, I'm sure that's the plan. But let me tell you from experience that if anything is going to go wrong, it'll go wrong in the kitchen."

According to the brochures, the entire island was only five miles long. But the roads had been designed to avoid spoiling the woodlands, and it took another fifteen minutes of winding twists and turns to reach the parking lot of the Seagrass Inn. A doorman stood beneath the entrance awning. "Now *this* is what I call luxury," Amelia exclaimed, drinking in the view as Peggy drove around the building.

The beach nearby was amazingly uncrowded for a Fourth of July weekend—probably, Amelia presumed, because the four beachfront-resort hotels were set so far apart. Children played in the surf while their parents sunbathed.

Amelia took off her sunglasses and nodded approvingly. "Nice," she said. "Really nice."

Peggy drove slowly along the road that overlooked the beach. "I guess each hotel has its own lounge and restaurant. Look—an open-air cabana, 'Entertainment Nightly.' Maybe if there's nothing on the schedule tonight we'll come back and do a little dancing."

Amelia smiled wryly. Peggy could walk into any club in the country and have someone ask her to dance within three minutes; while Amelia could walk into the same club and within three minutes be ready to leave.

She had spent most of her life expecting rejection. Until her junior year in college she had been fat, introverted and—as she often remarked to herself when she looked at old photographs—about as exciting as cottage cheese. Now she was a perfect size eight and had learned how to make the most of clothes and makeup. Though she had a great deal more self-confidence than she'd had at age twenty, still, when she looked in the mirror, all she saw was a mouth that was too wide, a nose too sprinkled with freckles, and eyes a nondescript hazel. Having long since accepted the fact that nothing would make her beautiful, she was always startled when someone suggested she was attractive. Unlike Peggy, she never felt comfortable in social situations. And that was only one of the reasons she preferred to spend the weekend lying on the beach with a good book to playing a mystery game with a group of strangers.

She craned her neck as Peggy made the turn that took them away from the resort area. At least, she reassured herself, if things got too bad she knew how to get to the beach for some peace and quiet.

"All right," Peggy said. "Now you've seen the beach, finish reading about the plantation."

Reluctantly Amelia turned her attention back to the brochure in her hand. "'Aury Island has a long and colorful history,'" she read. "'Stories of hauntings, mysterious disappearances, strange lights and unusual magnetic effects have prompted modern-day parapsychologists to speculate that the plantation may be located on one of the earth's 'hot spots'—a gravitational center that, during certain atmospheric conditions, is reputedly capable of generating unusual phenomena.'"

Amelia pushed up her glasses and gave her friend a dry look. "Great. You sure know how to pick a vacation spot, don't you?"

Peggy grinned. "Like the publicity lady said, this place has everything. Go on."

Amelia scanned the brochure until she found her place again. "'Although the history of the plantation is rife with tales of high romance and dark mystery, the murder of Sam Calvert is the most notorious incident. He was shot to death in the west garden of the estate on the night of July 4, 1870. The apparent motive for the shooting was the theft of a diamond-and-ruby necklace belonging to Calvert's stepmother. Although the suspect was never apprehended, eyewitnesses cast the blame on Jeffrey Craig, the oldest son and heir to the estate. Craig fled, presumably for Western territories, and neither he nor the stolen necklace were ever seen again.''

"Is that it?" Peggy asked. "That's the mystery we're supposed to act out this weekend?"

"Doesn't seem like much of a mystery," Amelia agreed, "if we already know who did it. Wait—it says here that debate over Jeffrey Craig's guilt or innocence became a cause célèbre in the South Carolina lowlands for many years and eventually everyone who was present at the estate that weekend became a suspect." She shrugged. "So I guess the answer to who-did-it will depend on whoever wrote the script."

"Well, you've got to admit, it's pretty clever to use a *real* murder mystery for one of these weekends. Wouldn't it be something if we could actually solve the crime after all these years?"

Amelia stuffed the brochures back into her tote bag. "After all these years, who cares? Besides, I think Craig did it. Otherwise, eyewitnesses wouldn't have said he did."

"Eyewitnesses have been wrong before. Besides, it's never the most obvious suspect—otherwise, what would be the point?"

Amelia didn't say—though she would have liked to—that as far as she could tell, there *was* no point to this entire weekend. Since she had come this far, she might as well be a good sport about it. At least she now knew where the beach was. . . .

A small cedar-shingle sign with an arrow pointing right announced Aury Island Plantation, and Peggy made the turn onto a smooth blacktop surface that was even narrower than the one they had been traveling. Stately oaks and cypresses lined the road on either side, and the undergrowth had been trimmed back to parklike preciseness. Through the clearing Amelia got an occasional glimpse of plowed fields and pastureland. She tapped Peggy on the arm. "Look—they're actually using a mule-drawn plow!"

"It's supposed to be a replica of a working plantation," Peggy reminded her. "Like Salem or Williamsburg. You know—history in motion."

"I wonder if all the food they serve is grown here," Amelia mused. "Now *that* would be worth writing about. And if they use organic farming methods or chemicals... 'From Field To Table,'" she said, drawing a line in the air as though to underline the title. "'Dining As It Was Meant To Be.'"

Peggy grinned. "And a sidebar—'Were Our Ancestors Really Healthier—Or Just Fatter?'"

"Do you know how long it's been since I've had a really good tomato?" Amelia settled back in her seat with a blissful smile on her face. "Maybe this won't be such a bad weekend, after all."

The car rounded a curve, and the plantation house came into view. Amelia sat up a little straighter. She had to admit it *was* striking—though not much like the Hollywood version of an authentic antebellum mansion. It was a pale yellow, three-story, U-shaped structure with a red-tile roof, surrounded by upper and lower verandas and floor-to-ceiling windows that glinted in the late-afternoon sun. The verandas were supported by a series of white columns, but the over-all effect was more comfortable than palatial. She had come here expecting Tara, but this mansion was more in the style of the West Indies than the Old South.

The paved drive gave way to a circular gravel entrance surrounded by an emerald lawn, which was separated from the plowed fields beyond by a split-rail fence. "Be careful where you step," Amelia warned when she noticed the herd of sheep evidently responsible for the clipped appearance of the grass. Then she laughed in delight as a peacock strutted out from behind a corner of the building. Obviously the brochure hadn't lied when it claimed that no detail had been spared in the recreation of an authentic, working plantation.

A deeply tanned young blond man in a nineteenth-century frock coat and trousers came running up to open the doors for them as Peggy pulled the car to a stop before the house. "Welcome to Aury Island Plantation," he said, smiling. "Registration is right up those stairs in the front hall. Is your luggage in the trunk?"

"We were told not to bring much," Peggy answered, handing him the keys.

He grinned. "Yes, ma'am. The hotel is providing costumes for the weekend. I'll take your car on out to the garage. You won't be needing it while you're here. Ya'll have a nice stay, now."

"Does it ever make you feel weird to be called 'ma'am' by a guy who looks like somebody you used to date?" Peggy murmured as the young man got behind the wheel and drove off.

Amelia chuckled. "They *are* getting younger, aren't they?"

She pushed her sunglasses up on her head and looked around. The sky was beginning to cloud over, and the sun flitted in and out, sporadically deepening the richness of the greenery and the vibrance of the yellow, orange and red flowers that were attractively arranged in terra-cotta planters around the drive. Despite the heat and the oppressive humidity, there was something soothing, even alluring, about the vista.

"It's nice," Peggy commented, hitching the strap of her canvas travel tote over her shoulder. "Reminds me of St. Thomas, in a way."

"Well," Amelia admitted, "I like the peacocks. But it sure is hot. I hope this mystery takes place in the air-conditioned house."

"It looks like it's going to rain. That'll cool things off. I love island storms." With her typical exuberance, Peggy started up the stairs.

Amelia, feeling wilted and sticky and just a bit envious of her friend's energy, smoothed out her wrinkled shorts and followed.

TWO

Double doors opened into a cool, dark foyer that was as spacious as a small ballroom. There were vases of cut flowers before the windows and beside each of the twin curving staircases; a stately grandfather clock ticked off the minutes with the steady swing of its brass pendulum. A discreet black board listing the schedule of activities was mounted on an easel just inside the doorway, but that was the only sign of modern life in the otherwise perfectly restored interior. Despite herself, Amelia was impressed.

Three or four people stood chatting around the left-hand staircase, and a white-coated waiter hovered nearby with a tray of drinks. As Amelia and Peggy entered, a tall woman with short salt-and-pepper hair came toward them, her hand extended.

"You must be Miss Brewer and Miss Langston," she said warmly. "We'd just about given up on you ladies. You didn't get lost, I hope."

Peggy explained how they had decided to explore the island and Amelia gave the management points for providing personal attention to their guests. Of course, that wouldn't be hard to do when those guests were a select group of individuals who, by their written or spoken criticism, could make or break a new hotel.

"Well, I'm glad you made it with no trouble," the woman was saying with a smile. "I'm Karen Striker, and I'll be your hostess this weekend. Let's just step over to the desk and get you checked in. Everyone else has already arrived."

Check-in consisted of literally checking their names off a list and handing them each an embossed folder that, Karen explained, contained information about the events scheduled for the weekend and the roles they had been assigned to play in the drama. As Karen handed them each a separate, smaller envelope containing a room key and a map of the plantation house and its surroundings, she reminded them that the first one to successfully solve the mystery would be awarded a magnum of champagne, a two-hundred-dollar cash prize, and an assortment of gift certificates from island shops.

"But we already know who did it," Amelia pointed out. "Jeffrey Craig."

Karen's eyes twinkled. "Did he? He was never found, you know, and neither was the murder weapon. We may have a few surprises in store for you this weekend, Miss Langston, so stay on your toes."

Karen led the way toward the stairs where a stocky gray-haired man in a business suit was avidly discussing real-estate prices with two middle-aged women who looked like they wanted nothing more than to get out of their high-heeled shoes. "We're very proud of the restoration work that has been done here," Karen said. "Most of the house is just as you would have found it in 1870—except, of course, that bathrooms have been added to all of the guest rooms, and the third floor, which used to be servants' quarters, has been converted into suites. But all of that was done without tampering with the architectural integrity of the house or changing the outer facade in the least. And of course we were very careful to preserve the historical artifacts we found when the work was undertaken. On the west side of the house, for example, you'll find that part of the brick has been chipped away from the chimney—supposedly from the bullet that struck and killed Sam Calvert. Be sure to take a look at it when you're in the west garden." She tossed a smile over her shoulder. "Maybe a little forensic detective work will help you solve the mystery."

Though it was obviously a rehearsed speech, Karen delivered it with such warmth and enthusiasm that Amelia found herself being drawn in. "Are these portraits of the Craigs?" she asked, gesturing toward the heavily framed pictures that lined the upper parts of both staircases.

"That's right. It's not a complete collection, of course. When the house was closed up in 1945, most of the artwork was stored in the attic—not very well, I might add—and a lot of it was lost to weather and rodents. But what you see now is a fair representation of what was here in 1870—with one notable exception." She paused and gestured across the foyer to the opposite staircase. "That third portrait there is of Martha Craig, Jeffrey Craig's mother. It wasn't painted until 1879, but we were so fortunate to find it we felt it had to have a place of honor among the others.

"Speaking of Martha Craig," Karen went on, "she's the one who designed the gardens much as you see them today. Some people have called them the

most beautiful gardens in the Southeast, which is quite
an honor when you consider the competition. Formal
gardens such as these were also quite unusual in the
South at this time, for on a working plantation everything was designed to have a useful purpose. But
Martha Craig is quoted as saying, 'The only difference between civilization and barbarism is a garden.'
I hope you'll make time to enjoy her efforts while
you're here."

Peggy wanted to know how long Karen had been
working at the plantation, and Karen revealed that she
was distantly related to the original Craigs. She had
gotten involved with the restoration and had stayed on
as publicity manager and director of special events.
Amelia's attention wandered to the view from the sec-
ond-story window, which revealed a beautifully arranged garden of wildflowers and, beyond it, a long
low building enclosed by shutters. It reminded Amelia of an old-fashioned bathhouse, but she didn't see
a pool in evidence.

She was just about to inquire about a swimming
pool when Karen stopped and opened a door. "Here
you are. This was one of the original family rooms—
the oldest sister's, I believe. Your costumes for the
weekend are waiting for you, and you should be able
to find everything else you need."

Peggy and Amelia exchanged a surprised, gratified
look. The room was huge, the ceilings at least four-
teen feet high, the hardwood floors a polished ma-
hogany. Two French windows were draped with lace
curtains, the four-poster beds canopied in a gossamer
fall of mosquito netting. The walls were papered in a
light spring-green print, the beds covered with deli-

cate white crocheted counterpanes. There were twin armoires against the walls, a skirted dressing table, and a marble fireplace with a delicate rose-embroidered fire screen. It was both elegant and romantic—far beyond anything Amelia had expected. She drew in a breath and barely suppressed a very unsophisticated, "Wow!"

Karen smiled at their silent reaction and touched a wall switch that illuminated twin fixtures cleverly disguised to look like gas lamps. "I hope you'll be comfortable. If you need anything..." She walked over to a velvet bellpull suspended between the beds and touched it lightly. "Just pull this. We're on an intercom system here, and someone will answer your request the minute you make it. Now..." She glanced at her watch. "We're all going to meet for welcome cocktails and a briefing about the weekend's events at six in the rose garden. That should give you just enough time to get settled and change into your costumes."

She started toward the door and then turned back, her eyes twinkling conspiratorially. "Oh, and I should tell you that we have hired actors to play some of the key parts, so we're asking that everyone keep his or her real identity secret until the mystery is solved. If you knew who was an actor and who was a regular guest, you might have an edge on the mystery, right? So try to stay in character until Sunday night."

She opened the door and advised with a friendly wave, "Remember, if you need anything, our staff is just a bellpull away."

When Karen had closed the door behind her, Amelia said it: "Wow!"

"Bellpulls, can you believe it? Is this luxury or what? I wonder if they send a maid to lace up your corset?"

"Look at this furniture, will you? It must have cost a fortune. I don't believe anybody could really afford to live like this in 1870."

"Why not? When you own an island you can pretty much live as you please." Peggy walked across the room and opened a door. "Amy, you should see this bathroom! It's huge." She came out of the bathroom, grinning broadly. "This is one of those times I'm glad I didn't listen to my mother and become a dentist. The perks of this job are unbelievable! All dentists get are free false teeth. Now, aren't you glad you're not staying in some pseudo-Caribbean-beachfront room just like the thousands of other pseudo-Carribean-beachfront rooms in hotels across America?"

"Well, I don't know...." Amelia fingered the silky texture of the mosquito netting, though she was suppressing a smile of her own. "There's no television. And—" she looked around "—no telephone."

"God, you are impossible." Peggy flung herself down on the bed, raising an arm dramatically to her forehead. "You know what the trouble with you is? No sense of adventure. You're so bogged down in routine you can't even appreciate a change when you stumble right over it. Breakfast at eight, dinner at six o'clock. You miss one night of 'Star Trek' reruns and your whole week is thrown off."

"Hey, I like 'Star Trek,'" Amelia objected. "It's educational." But what she should have said was "reassuring." Peggy was right; she did take comfort in the familiar. She enjoyed routine and scheduled her life around things she could count on, and she liked it that way. Mrs. Paul's frozen dinners never let her down. Captain James T. Kirk always managed to pull one last trick out of his hat to save the day. News at six, movie at eleven, life went on. And when a lover said goodbye and a career went down the drain, it was nice to know that some things didn't change. So she liked a little stability in her life. What was wrong with that?

Shaking away the sudden melancholy that had engulfed her, Amelia turned toward the window. "It *is* a nice room," she said. "Great view. What do you suppose that building over there is? The one that looks like a pool house?"

Peggy sat up. "You know," she said seriously, "if you'd let it, this weekend could be the best thing in the world for you. You need a break, a chance to get away and put things in perspective. A time to not *think* so much. You know what I mean?"

Amelia smiled a little and turned back to Peggy. "Yeah, I guess you're right. I have been kind of a drag lately, haven't I?"

Peggy shrugged. "You're entitled. But try to loosen up for a few days, okay? Meet some new people, get into the spirit of things, have fun."

"Well," Amelia said brightly, "in for a penny, in for a pound, I guess. And here we are with no television and no telephone—I guess we might as well have fun." Or at least, she amended to herself, pretend to have fun.

"That's the attitude."

Amelia sat on the edge of her bed and opened the packet Karen had given her. "However," she warned

Peggy, "if it gets too weird you won't get mad, will you, if I sneak off to the beach?"

Peggy grinned. "If I find that cute-looking parking attendant, will you get mad if I don't come back to the room tonight?"

"He's a child!"

"If he's as good as he looks, I might not come back all weekend."

Amelia groaned. "I remember Aruba." On that particular trip, Peggy had met a blackjack dealer and Amelia had seen her exactly twice during the week-long trip—once when they checked into their room and once when they checked out. That was actually one of the reasons Amelia liked traveling with Peggy— she had all the privacy she needed.

"So, what have you got?" Peggy opened up her packet.

Amelia separated the pieces of literature until she found the card that read "You have been assigned to play the role of..." She made a wry face as she read aloud, "'The mysterious stranger.' Great. I don't even get a real name. I guess they ran out of parts before they ran out of people." She shrugged and tucked the card back into the folder. "At least it won't be hard to play. I don't have to do anything."

"I don't know. In all the mystery novels I've read, the mysterious stranger is always the one who did it. Well, will you look at this?" She held up her own card with a smug look of triumph. "You are looking at the new-and-improved Miss Abigail Craig, sister of the accused and no doubt a major player in the drama to come."

"How come you get to be a Craig and I don't even get a name?"

"Luck of the draw, babe." Peggy scrambled off the bed and over to the armoires. "Let's look at our costumes."

With the exception of two truly stunning ball gowns—one in peach taffeta and the other in green silk—the costumes were something of a disappointment. They were either cotton or sturdy muslin in plain checks and prints, with high necks and long sleeves. Amelia grimaced. "They look like something my grandmother would wear."

Peggy gave her a dry look and Amelia grinned. "I guess there's a reason for that. So, how do we know which dress is for who?"

"See what fits, I guess. We gave them our sizes, remember? I wonder if we dress for dinner." She pulled out the frothy green gown.

"I think that's for the party, Saturday night. Look at this!" She pulled out what appeared to be a folded cartwheel covered with muslin from the bottom drawer of the wardrobe. "I didn't know they still wore hoop skirts in 1870!"

"It's not a hoop. It's a bustle. Look." Peggy held the whalebone-reinforced undergarment up to her waist and giggled. "Imagine anybody *wanting* her backside to look this big! But look at these darling little slippers! Can you believe the money they spent on these costumes? Oh, this *is* going to be fun!" She gathered up petticoat, slippers and a brown-and-yellow dress from a hook at the back of the wardrobe. "I'm going to shower and change—I can't wait to see what I look like!"

The one thing Amelia didn't like about traveling with Peggy was her tendency to hog the bathroom. By the time she came out, complaining about the buttons she couldn't reach on the back of her gown and trying to pin up her hair, it was a quarter to six. Amelia helped Peggy with the buttons and decided to postpone her own shower until later that evening.

While Peggy fussed in front of the mirror with a curling iron, trying to coax her hair into a collection of ringlets like the ones she'd seen in costume dramas on television, Amelia slipped into her own gown. The dress she had chosen was white cotton with a rosebud print, and it didn't look nearly as bad on Amelia as it had on the wardrobe hanger. The skirt was fuller and more graceful than the hobble skirts one usually associated with bustles—which she vaguely thought might have been worn later in the century—and draped so elegantly at the back that she didn't look nearly as ridiculous as she had expected. It had a long bodice that buttoned up the front, and was trimmed with a narrow band of cotton lace around the front closure, as were the square neckline and the three-quarter-length puffed sleeves. Pink ribbon drawstrings formed a ruffle on the sleeves, and when Amelia tried to adjust the tie on the left sleeve, the ribbon pulled completely out.

"Oh, no." She looked at it in dismay. "Do you have a safety pin?"

"Maybe you should pick another dress." Peggy glanced at her watch. "It's already six."

"It'll be faster to fix this one." Amelia began to unbutton the bodice while Peggy scrambled through her purse for a sewing kit.

Peggy grinned as Amelia, in the white cotton chemise she had worn under her shorts top, flipped her long hair over one shoulder and sat on the bed, the long skirt billowing around her. "You look just like one of those old-fashioned paintings," she said. "*Young Girl Sewing.* I always did say there was a lot of the Southern belle in you at heart. What about me? How do I look?"

Amelia glanced up as Peggy twirled around, showing a great deal of petticoat and more ankle than any self-respecting woman of the nineteenth century would ever have dared. "Take off the watch," Amelia suggested.

"Oh, right." Peggy looked at the big, black-banded watch and giggled. "I guess it does kind of spoil the effect. Are you going to be much longer?"

Amelia fastened the safety pin to the ribbon and squinted as she threaded it through the sleeve casing. "Maybe you'd better go on ahead. One of us should be there in case they tell us anything important."

"I don't want to leave you...."

"I'll be right behind you."

"Well, okay."

Amelia could tell Peggy's reluctance was only pro forma as she searched through the papers scattered on her bed for the plantation map. "The rose garden, right? You won't be long?"

"I just have to do my hair."

"All right, then. I'll see you down there."

When Peggy closed the door behind her, Amelia muffled a sigh of relief. She really wasn't in any hurry to get downstairs. With any luck the party would be well under way by the time she got there and she could fade quietly into the background.

She finished threading the ribbon, tied it securely, and slipped on the bodice. Standing before the cheval mirror, she buttoned up the garment and was surprised at the woman she saw there. One good thing had to be said for nineteenth-century fashions: They might be hot, heavy and uncomfortable, but they were definitely flattering. The narrow bodice made her waist look almost nonexistent, and the modest neckline that came to just below the collarbone would make even the most undistinguished bosom look appealing. The ribbons that trailed from the elbow-length ruffle of the sleeve added a bit of romance. With an approving nod into the mirror, she fastened the last button and began to work on her hair.

She had no intention of spending as much time fussing with a curling iron as Peggy had—not in this humidity, anyway—so she parted her hair straight down the middle and coiled it tightly away from her face on either side, fastening each section securely with bobby pins. As a finishing touch, she tied a pink ribbon around her hair so that it formed a band from crown to nape. The hairstyle flattered her heart-shaped face, and she was surprised at how perfectly in character she looked. Peggy was right—she could have posed for one of those portraits of an old-fashioned girl.

After a moment's hesitation, she took off her wristwatch and used the safety pin to fasten it inconspicuously to the inside of her bodice. It was a Rolex timepiece—a graduation gift from her grandmother and the only piece of really expensive jewelry she owned, and she didn't want to leave it in the room. She left her necklace—a gold initial pendant her mother had given her for her birthday—on, tucking it beneath the neckline of her dress. After one last look in the mirror, she left the room.

She was halfway down the stairs when she realized she had forgotten both her room key and her plantation map. She stifled an oath, but it was hard to remember things like that when one didn't carry a purse, and there was nothing she could do about it now. She only hoped Peggy had remembered her key; if not, they would have a chance to find out just how efficient the staff of Aury Plantation was.

The foyer was deserted, so there was no one from whom Amelia could request directions. She looked around uncertainly, then started for the front door.

The sky had darkened considerably, and the air was hot and still. She could already feel her hair starting to frizz. She turned to the left, following the angle of the building until she came upon a gravel path that curved slightly away from the house and toward an arrangement of tall, trimmed evergreen bushes that looked as though they shielded a garden. Thinking she heard voices from that direction, she followed the path.

But once she entered the shelter of the spruce shrubs, she realized she could no longer hear the voices. She was in a garden, all right; the evergreens formed a semicircular enclosure at the center of which was a brick fountain surrounded by a colorful planting of pink and yellow columbine. A willow tree grew near the fountain, under which were two white wrought-iron benches. Nearby was a flagstone patio covered by a wooden pavilion. It was all very charming; quiet, isolated, and the ideal spot for a romantic rendezvous or to be alone with one's thoughts—but it was obviously the wrong garden.

She looked around. She could see the eaves of the house to her right, and, through a break in the spruce bushes, an outbuilding of some sort to the left. Since, as she recalled, the house was U-shaped, if she continued walking in the same direction she should eventually cover the entire grounds. Or so she hoped.

She started forward again, and her attention was caught by the chimney. On impulse, she went over to it.

She bent close, running her fingers over the age-smoothed brick, until she found it: a very definite, slashing scar of chipped brick at about the height of her shoulders.

"Well, well," she murmured. "The very bullet mark." And even though she wasn't normally a superstitious person, Amelia felt a prickle of dread. A man had been murdered here, on the very ground where she stood. Blood had soaked the ground, and if she were quiet enough and still enough, she could almost hear the echo of the explosion that had split the night.

It took Amelia a moment to realize that what she was hearing was the roll of distant thunder. She looked up worriedly at the sky, which was dark with purplish thunderclouds. No wonder she was spooked. Weather like this could set anyone's nerves on edge.

At least she knew where she was—in the west garden. She picked up her skirts and hurried on, listening for the voices that would guide her to the party. The winding gravel path forked, and a sudden gust of wind brought the sound of a woman's laughter. She thought the sound came from the right, so she went in that direction. The air was heavy with the scent of magnolias, and a huge tree hid the house from her view. The sky was growing darker, and Amelia walked faster. Around her were attractive oval-shaped beds of bright red and pink begonias, the blossoms shaken by the breeze that came in stronger gusts and had the definite taste of rain to it.

"This is ridiculous," Amelia muttered. By the time she found the rose garden—if she ever did—the party would have moved inside. The best thing she could do would be to go back to the house before she got soaked.

She paused, looking around to get her bearings, and a flash of lightning illuminated the sky. This was going to be a severe storm, and she had no desire to be caught out in it.

There was a clearing just up ahead, in the center of which sat a stone sundial. She started toward it, hoping that from there she would at least be able to see the house and find the shortest route back.

By the time she reached the clearing the gloom was so intense she could barely see the gravel path behind her. The wind bent the tops of the trees and tugged at her skirts, and the sky had a peculiar yellow-green tint to it. She wondered if this was what a hurricane looked like.

Still moving toward the sundial, she strained her neck backward, trying to catch a glimpse of the house through the wildly waving branches of the trees. She could almost smell lightning in the air, and the static electricity was so strong it prickled her skin. Shivering, she rubbed her arms and took another step forward.

She gasped out loud as her skirt was flung up to her waist. Stumbling backward, she attempted to push it down again but the material clung to her hands as if imbued with a magnetic charge. She could *feel* that charge all around her, prickling at her scalp, making the hairs on the backs of her arms stand straight up. A bolt of panic went through her as she realized what was happening—she had heard of people reporting phenomena like this just before they were struck by lightning.

Choking back a cry, she stumbled toward the sundial, trying to get away from the trees that would act like lightning rods in a storm. And suddenly the air felt as thick as molasses, hot and dry and practically crackling with electricity. It was actually difficult to walk. She felt as though she was pushing against some unseen force with every step she took; the front of her skirt was pressed hard and flat against her legs, hampering her movements. And though she could see the wind whipping the leaves back and forth from white to dark green to white again, she couldn't feel it. This was no ordinary storm.

And she couldn't hear anything—not the roar of the wind, not the rustle of the leaves—not anything at all except a faint, low humming, like the sound that was made by a powerful electrical generator. *My God,* she thought, looking around in wonder. *My God...*

There was a fierce tingling in her legs and arms, as if a thousand ants were crawling all over her skin. Her heart was pounding and her throat was dry and she backed farther away from the trees, certain that any moment she was about to be struck by lightning. But the closer she got to the sundial, the more pronounced the bizarre effects became.

She suddenly felt a tearing sensation in her hair and her hands flew to her head as the bobby pins were ripped out of place. In horror, she watched as the metal pins shot through the air like arrows and landed against the face of the stone sundial. Then she understood. She didn't believe it, but she understood. The sundial was somehow magnetically charged. *This* was one of those "hot spots" the brochure had talked about—it had to be. And she had stumbled right into it.

"Oh...my...God..." Her voice sounded tinny and hollow, and she took a hesitant step toward the sundial. The moment she did, her loosened hair began to fly around her head and her skirts stood straight out again. A strange exhilaration went through her—a thrill of wonder and excitement—and she took a step closer. She had to tell the others. Somebody had to *see* this. And quickly, before it stopped.

She shouted, "Hey! Somebody—anybody! Come here! You won't believe this!"

She could hardly hear her own voice above the buzzing, humming sound that charged the air, and she turned and started to run. But she had forgotten about the long skirts she wore.

Her toe caught the edge of her skirt and she pitched forward. She flung out her arm to catch the edge of the sundial, and the next thing she knew there was a sharp explosion of pain in her head, a sensation of falling and a terrible nausea. Then, cold blackness engulfed her.

THREE

Amelia opened her eyes to a blurred image that reminded her of a face—green eyes, the shape of a shadowed jaw, a wave of jet hair. In the distance she heard a low, soothing voice murmuring, "There you go. Take a deep breath. You're going to be all right."

Obeying the note of calm authority in the voice, she took a deep breath, and another. Gradually the dizziness dispersed, leaving only a queasy feeling and a mild headache. She swallowed hard and focused her eyes.

It *was* a man bending over her. His face was a coppery color—the shade naturally tanned skin acquires when it has been exposed to the sun once too often. His jawline was square and distinct, and when he smiled, as he did now, faint lines appeared around his mouth and radiated from the corners of his eyes. Amelia saw all this very clearly and in vivid detail, but that was all she saw. She was lying on the ground, that much she knew, but she couldn't feel the grass beneath her or see the sky above. She couldn't remember how she had gotten there or why she felt so sick and weak. All she could do was stare into the face looking down at her, wondering why such an incredibly handsome man was kneeling on the ground and patting her wrist.

"How do you feel?" he inquired gently. "Any better?"

She moaned and tried to sit up. Nauseated, she sank back down again. "No," she managed faintly. "I feel awful."

"All right, just lie still." He turned his head and shouted, "Mother!"

The volume of the shout made her squeeze her eyes closed. When she opened them again he was still there, chafing her wrist between his hands. Weakly, she pulled her hand away. "What happened?" she moaned.

"I thought you could tell me." He sat back on his heels, bracing his hands against his thighs, looking down at her with a mixture of sympathy and amusement. "I came around the corner and there you were, crumpled beneath the sundial. It was rather startling, let me tell you."

Then Amelia remembered the storm, the crazy way the bobby pins had jumped out of her hair, then running to tell the others . . . and falling. "Oh, how embarrassing," she muttered. "I tripped over my skirts and must have hit my head...." Gingerly, she touched her forehead; and sure enough, a lump was beginning to rise just beneath the hairline.

Wincing, she tried to sit up, but the firm pressure of his hands on her shoulders pushed her back again. "Just stay put," he advised her. "No point in having you swoon all over again." He called out again, "Mother!"

"Good gracious! What is all this—"

Amelia turned her head to see a plump, middle-aged woman in period costume round the path, followed by a younger woman, also in costume. The first woman stopped with her hand at her throat when she saw Amelia lying there on the ground. "Gracious!" she exclaimed, and hurried toward her. "What on earth has happened?"

"This young lady seems to have swooned in our garden, Mother," the man replied politely, and stood aside to allow his mother room. "I thought you'd want to know."

"Oh, you poor dear!" Gathering up her mauve skirts to pad her knees, the woman sank beside Amelia, a worried look on her face.

Amelia struggled to her elbows, embarrassed by all the attention. "I'm all right, really. I just tripped and fell, but I'm not really hurt—"

"Why, you're as white as a sheet!" The older woman laid a smooth hand against Amelia's cheek. "And clammy, too— My dear, don't you know you should never go out in this sun without a hat? Abigail, run into the house and tell Lotti to soak some towels in spring water. Jeff, come help her inside. My word, such a day as this isn't fit for man or beast. It's a wonder we're not all overcome."

The younger woman hurried away, and Amelia noticed then that the sun *was* shining, and it was stifling hot, when only moments ago a storm had been brewing. How long had she been unconscious? The dark-haired man came toward her and Amelia noticed for the first time that he, too, was dressed in period costume, and she was mortified to have spoiled the party, not to mention having to meet all these people for the first time in such inauspicious circumstances.

"Please, really, I'm all right," she protested quickly as the man knelt beside her and it became clear he intended to pick her up. "I can walk, really, you don't have to...."

He lifted her effortlessly into his arms and there was nothing Amelia could do but give a weak, apologetic smile, then quickly turn her face against his broadcloth-clad shoulder to hide her embarrassment.

But even though the circumstances were something less than ideal, she had to admit there was something... well, thrilling about being carried by such a strong, attractive stranger. And he was strong—not in the overstated musclebulging way of a bodybuilder, but like a man who worked for a living. His arms were firm around her, his shoulders tight, his stride long and easy. And when at last he laid her on a small, humpbacked couch in a cool room, he wasn't even flushed with exertion.

"Th-thank you," Amelia murmured, and the smooth way in which he cocked one eyebrow at her made her avoid his gaze. Her hand went to her hair, which was windblown and scattered around her shoulders. "I must look a mess."

"You look just fine," he said, and gave a polite, quaintly old-fashioned little bow from the waist. But there was a trace of something resembling lazy curiosity in his eyes that made Amelia feel as though she had something to hide—which was ridiculous, because she didn't.

The older woman was moving about the room, methodically closing the wooden blinds. "What I don't understand," she said, "is how she got into our garden in the first place. Will you please explain to me, Jeffrey, how a perfectly nice young lady can wander into our garden and swoon dead away without anyone knowing about it at all?"

Propping herself into a half-sitting position on the slippery horsehair sofa, Amelia turned to look at her. "Well, I got lost, and it was the strangest thing—there was a storm, or at least I thought it was a storm, and there was so much electricity in the air that I could actually feel it on my skin. And then all the bobby pins were just pulled out of my hair as if by a magnet, and I called out for somebody to see, but then when I started to run I tripped and—"

About halfway through the story, Amelia knew she had made a mistake. Peggy might have believed her, but who did she think she was, telling this bizarre story to two strangers?

The woman had stopped closing the blinds and had turned to stare at her. Amelia didn't dare look at the man. She focused instead on a grass stain on her skirt, trying to rub it out with her fingers. "Well," she mumbled, "I guess it's really not important."

"The heat," announced the woman decisively. "I once knew a young girl who was delirious for three weeks from it. Took to her bed for the rest of the summer and never did completely recover—still a little touched in the head, you know. Not," she added hastily, "that anything like that would ever happen to you, my dear. We simply won't allow it—"

"I brought some cold buttermilk, Mama." The younger woman entered the room, a silver platter containing a white pitcher and glasses in her hands. "And Lotti is getting the towels. How is she?"

"Oh, good!" The older woman hurried forward and poured a glass of the thick white substance from the pitcher. "This will fix you right up. You just drink it down.... Not too fast, now. Just take it easy."

Amelia tried to keep her dislike from showing on her face as she reluctantly accepted the glass. She took a small, cautious sip and almost gagged at the sour, curdled taste.

"What I don't understand," said the older woman with a worried frown on her brow, "is how you got here, and—please don't think me impolite, my dear— but who *are* you?"

Amelia gratefully seized the opportunity to put the glass of buttermilk aside. She extended her hand. "No, I'm the one who was rude. I should have introduced myself earlier, and after you've been so nice... I'm Amelia Langston."

The woman looked at her proffered hand for a moment as though she wasn't quite sure what Amelia expected her to do with it. Then she took Amelia's hand between both of hers in a warm, brief clasp and said, "And I am Martha Craig, as you no doubt already know. My son, Jeffrey..."

The man bowed. "A pleasure, Miss Langston."

"And my daughter, Abigail."

The young woman who had brought in the buttermilk gave a bobbing curtsy, and Amelia stared at her. Her hair was chestnut-colored, her eyes blue, and she couldn't have been more than nineteen years old. Everyone else had used their assigned names—which Amelia thought was taking a good thing a little too far under the circumstances—but this was definitely not Peggy.

She said, "I thought Peggy was supposed to play Abigail."

The two women exchanged a confused look, and then a black woman entered bearing a stack of towels. "Lotti, thank goodness!" exclaimed the woman who called herself Martha Craig.

"I guess Peggy must have switched roles with someone at the party," Amelia murmured to herself. Or maybe she had found the parking-lot attendant and had given the role away. That made Amelia smile, but the smile quickly turned to a gasp of shock as her forehead was plastered with an ice-cold wet towel.

She sat upright and tried to fling the towel off, but gentle hands pushed her down again, all the while applying other freezing towels to her throat and bare arms and across her waist.

"Now there, dear, you just lie back. We have to get your temperature down—"

"I don't have a temperature—I mean, fever. I'm fine, really. And these things are freezing!"

"Of course they are, dear. That's what will make you better—"

"No! Please!" Amelia flung off the last of the towels and sat up. Martha Craig took a shocked step backward, Abigail looked frightened, and there was a soft sound from the man who called himself Jeff, which sounded suspiciously like muffled laughter.

Pushing back her damp hair and trying to muster whatever shreds of dignity she had left, Amelia said calmly, "Look, I know you're only trying to help, but

I'm in no danger of heatstroke, I promise. I'm just fine, and what I'd really like to do is—"

"Landston!" Martha Craig exclaimed, her troubled expression clearing into a pleased glow. "Why, of course, you must be Charlotte Landston's daughter!" She turned to Abigail. "You remember my dear friend Charlotte, don't you, dear? From Charleston?"

Abigail started to make some reply, and Amelia corrected, "No, it's Langston." And then she stopped.

Of course. These were the professional actors Karen had mentioned, and they were just acting out the script. She considered the exercise inappropriate—after all, she *could* have been seriously hurt—but she had to admire the neat way in which they had worked her into the drama. Charlotte Landston's daughter from Charleston? An old family friend? She could live with that.

Martha Craig sat down beside her, grasping her hands warmly. "Why, I just can't imagine why your mother didn't write to say you were coming! Of course..." And her brow puckered a little in disturbance. "Postal service isn't what it used to be since the Yankees took over.... Well." Her expression cleared once again as she decided, "I'll just have to send one of my boys to tell her you've arrived safely. Now, you must tell me everything. How is your dear mother? Why, it's been years! And how long can you stay? It must be until after the Fourth, because we're to have a grand party here, with rockets that came all the way from Philadelphia! Now, where are your bags, child? We'll have them taken up right away and after you've rested, you and I can have a nice long chat."

Despite herself, Amelia was charmed. The woman was a professional through and through, and she had everything down pat. Amelia said, "Well, I left my bag with a boy—"

"Oh, dear!" Martha looked dismayed. "Don't tell me you had them sent ahead? That boy at the ferry station is so unreliable you may never see your things again. I must remember to have Elliot speak to someone about having him dismissed. But don't worry, dear." She squeezed Amelia's hands reassuringly. "Abigail has just scads of lovely frocks she never wears and will be happy to share with you, won't you, dear?"

Abigail, looking somewhat confused, managed a quick smile and said, "Yes, of course."

"Which will work out perfectly, since you'll be sharing Abigail's room. I'm afraid we have a full house for the rest of the summer, but there's nothing more joyous than a table filled with family and friends in these troubled times! Now, then." She rose abruptly, beaming. "Abigail will take you upstairs where you'll have a nice long rest before supper."

Amelia started to protest, "But I just—" And then she thought better of it. After having made such a fool of herself with these people, she wasn't sure she was up to meeting the rest of the cast and crew. Her head hurt, and it might be a good idea to just take an aspirin and skip the rest of the party. She could meet everyone at supper.

She stood and smiled at the actress playing Mrs. Craig. "You really are wonderful," she told her, and glanced around to include the other two. "All of you are."

Jeff didn't return her smile—in fact his expression, as he looked at her, was almost scowling—but Martha Craig blushed prettily. "Well, aren't you sweet? Now, go on with you. Upstairs and lie down. Abigail, don't you pester her with your chatter. Let her rest."

Amelia followed the younger woman out of the room on legs that were not quite as steady as she would have liked. Her headache had receded to a dull discomfort behind her left eye, but she still felt weak and a little disoriented—and thoroughly dismayed by the spectacle she had made of herself.

She said to the girl walking up the stairs in front of her, "You really don't have to go with me, you know. I can find my own way, and I've caused enough trouble already...."

The girl flashed her a quick, bright smile. "Don't be silly, I don't mind a bit. Besides, a person could get lost in this big old house by herself."

"I suppose." But Amelia's attention, as they reached the first landing, wasn't really on the girl's words. She was struck by a feeling of there being something odd, something out of place in the house since she had last seen it. At first she couldn't put her finger on it, but then she remembered.

"The pictures," she said, stopping to look down the staircase at the portraits hung on the wall alongside the staircase.

Abigail grimaced. "Yes, aren't they hideous? All those old people dressed in black—it makes me feel like I'm in a church all the time."

"But...they're different." Amelia studied the paintings, wishing she could remember exactly *what* was different about them. She hadn't really looked at

them all that closely the first time, but she could have
sworn there were far more portraits now than there
had been when she and Peggy had come up the stairs.
They seemed to be hung closer together, and she was
sure there were some faces she didn't recognize.

"There's one missing," she said. "Where is Martha Craig's portrait?"

Abigail laughed lightly. "Mama? Goodness, she'd
never have her portrait painted. She's always saying a
lady should be remembered in the flower of her
youth—not the way she really is."

Amelia drew a breath to argue, but Abigail had already started up the stairs again. After one more puzzled look toward the place on the wall where Martha
Craig's portrait should have been, Amelia followed.

Just as they reached the door to her room, Amelia
said, "Oh, wait, I forgot my—"

She had started to say "key," but Abigail turned the
handle and the door opened without a key. Abigail
gave her a questioning look, and Amelia only smiled
faintly. Apparently she had forgotten to lock the
door—which was not the first stupid mistake she had
made that day.

The room looked much the same as before, except
that the long windows were open to admit a fluttering
breeze through the lace curtains, and apparently the
maid had been in to straighten up. The information
packet she had left scattered on the bed was gone, and
so were her discarded clothes and her tote bag. Even
with the breeze it was rather warm and sticky, but apparently the air-conditioning didn't work with the
windows open.

Abigail said with a shy smile, "I do hope you'll stay a good long time. It's going to be so nice to have a girl my age to talk to."

Amelia was both flattered and amused by the compliment; she was at least ten years older than the other girl. Although, when Amelia thought about it, she didn't act as young as she looked.

Abigail went on earnestly, "I know it's not nice to say, because I do love him dearly, but since Jeff got back things have been—well—strained around here. Mother's been so nervous and Elliot's angry all the time and then there're the Calverts and *nobody* likes them, and— Oh!" She caught herself with a guilty look. "Mother warned me not to tire you and here I am talking your ear off. I'm sorry. You just have to tell me to hush. Jeff is always calling me a chatterbox, and he's right."

Amelia had some difficulty following the conversation until she realized they were still playing out a script. She had never been very good at that sort of thing, but it seemed she had no choice but to go along. She asked, looking around for her tote bag, "You said Jeff just got back? Where has he been?"

"Out west. It sounds terribly exciting, but..." Her expression grew guarded and she walked over to turn down one of the beds. "He won't talk to me about it. He doesn't talk to anybody, really, and that only makes things worse. Of course," she added, "when he came here he was ill and has only been up and about a few weeks now. We haven't really had a chance to get used to him again."

"Ill?" Amelia was surprised. He had certainly looked healthy enough to her. More than healthy.

Abigail flushed. "Injured, I should have said. Some nasty accident out west. But he's perfectly recovered now," she added quickly, and looked up again with an apologetic smile. "But I'm being a terrible hostess, telling you all these dreary family tales and boring you to death. Do you really live in Charleston?" she asked with a sudden spark of excitement in her eyes. "I've always thought it must be the most glamorous thing in the world to live in a big city like that. Tell me, what is it like?"

Amelia started to answer with the truth, but then remembered her role—which was quickly growing tiresome, and, if the truth be told, more than a little bizarre. Didn't these people ever call off the game?

She said cautiously, "Charleston is a charming town. But it's really not all that big."

Abigail replied dreamily, "Oh, it seems big to me. Anything would seem big when you've spent your whole life on an island. Tell me . . . is it really overrun with Yankees and sailors and—and bawdy houses, like Mama says?"

But that was too much. Amelia touched her forehead gingerly and tried to soften her words with a pleading smile. "Look, could we stop now? Just for a little while. This is really making my head ache, and—"

"Oh, I'm sorry!" Immediately, Abigail was all concern. "Please, you must lie down." She came over to take Amelia's arms, and Amelia neatly sidestepped her. "Can I get you anything?"

"Well, maybe an aspirin. I have some in my tote bag, but—" She opened the door to the bathroom and stopped, staring.

It wasn't a bathroom at all. It was a dark, low-ceilinged semicloset containing nothing but trunks, a dressmaker's dummy, and dusty hatboxes. The musty-smelling air testified to the fact that this was a room that was seldom opened.

Standing there, staring into that hot, dim enclosure, Amelia felt a wave of disorientation so strong that the floor actually seemed to tilt beneath her feet. She turned around quickly and looked at the room behind her as though to assure herself that it, too, hadn't disappeared. Then she looked back into the closet.

Abigail said, "Is something wrong?" Her voice sounded puzzled, but far away and insignificant.

Amelia couldn't answer. Her throat was as dry as the dusty air that surrounded her and her heart was pounding, echoing the pulsing pain in her head. There had been a bathroom here. She was sure of it. Peggy had spent almost forty minutes in it; Amelia had heard the shower running—hadn't she? How could a whole bathroom just disappear?

Abigail came over to her. "What is it? Are you looking for something?"

"The bathroom," Amelia managed hoarsely. She gestured toward the storage space. "Where's the bathroom?"

Abigail's brow knitted. "You want to take a bath? Shall I have some water brought up?"

Amelia stared at her for a long time. The girl didn't look as though she was joking. But then she was an actress. And the act, as far as Amelia was concerned, had gone on too long.

She looked into the closet one more time, then brought her fingers up to the pounding headache that had spread to her temples. "Something weird is going on here," she muttered.

She looked sharply at Abigail, and then around the room once more. "This *is* my room, isn't it?" she said.

Abigail looked startled. "Why, no. I mean, you're welcome, of course, but—it's my room."

Almost, Amelia breathed a sigh of relief. Of course. All the rooms looked the same. She hadn't really noticed where she was and she had never been very good with directions anyway. She said, "I think I'd better go to my own room."

She started for the door.

Abigail sounded hurt and confused. "But—this is the only room available. We have a lot of guests and...please." She extended her hand in entreaty. "Won't you lie down and rest?"

Trying her best to remain calm Amelia demanded, "Do you mean to tell me that they switched my room—*and* my roommate—without even telling me?"

Abigail stared at her dumbly.

"Well, don't *you* mind?" Amelia insisted. "I mean, you don't even know me!"

Abigail replied soothingly, "No, I don't mind in the least. I told you, I'm glad to have you. But, please, you shouldn't get so upset. After all, you're ill, and— Can't I bring you some tea or something?"

Amelia drew in a deep breath and pressed her fingers to both temples. The girl was right about one thing—she shouldn't get so upset. Amelia had never been one to make a scene, and whatever had happened wasn't the actress's fault. If anything, it was Amelia's fault for missing the briefing; and in any case she could get it straightened out with the right people later.

She said, "I need my tote bag."

Abigail backed quickly toward the door. "I'll try to find it for you."

Amelia smiled apologetically. "I'm sorry. I don't mean to be such a pain. It's just that my head really hurts. If you don't mind, maybe I could just lie down for a while and get this all straightened out later."

Abigail looked somewhat reassured by her change of tone. "I understand. I'll try to find your bags, but if you want to take off your skirt I'll see what Lotti can do about getting the grass stains out, and I'll lay out something for you to wear to supper."

"Thanks. That would be nice."

Amelia didn't intend to lie down at all. She had determined to go find Karen—or at the very least, her own room—as soon as the annoyingly persistent actress left. But her head was pounding so badly that she could hardly think, and she knew she wasn't up to dealing with a registration snafu just then. She wasn't even up to getting angry about it.

She stepped out of her skirt and put on a cotton wrapper Abigail had left for her—which Amelia didn't recall having seen in the wardrobe the first time she inspected it—and lay down on the bed. Staring up through the gauzy haze of mosquito netting, she counted off, in approximate order of importance, the things she had lost in the short time she had been here. Her roommate. A bathroom. Her tote bag. Her key and registration packet. What was next? Her sanity?

Damn you, Peggy! Why did I ever let you talk me into this?

This was supposed to be fun. A chance to get away from it all. Well, she was getting away from it all, all right. Right into the Twilight Zone.

Peggy would have said, of course, that that was just one of Amelia's problems—she took things too seriously, and she didn't know *how* to relax, and wouldn't know fun if it jumped up and bit her in the face. Peggy's advice would have been to just let loose and go with the flow.

And maybe she was right. The weekend had gotten off to a bad start, first with missing the party, then the accident, and now this mix-up with the rooms.... Maybe if she just gave it a chance, she could enjoy herself.

But Amelia didn't think so. The whole thing seemed entirely too weird.

FOUR

Amelia hadn't expected to sleep, and was surprised when she opened her eyes sometime later to a deep twilight. The room had cooled off some, and her headache was gone. She stretched and sat up, pushing her hair away from her face with her fingers, and she felt much better about the entire situation than she had before.

She still wasn't thrilled about being assigned to a room without a bathroom—she was an invited guest, after all, not one of the hired help. At least it was clear what had happened. Peggy must have switched roles with someone or skipped out altogether, and the management must have made some rearrangements in their room plans. Probably Peggy had forgotten to clear it with Amelia.

Even though Peggy had done some strange things before, it really wasn't like her to go this far. She had known Amelia hadn't wanted to come here in the first place, and she might at least have said something before abandoning her to a strange roommate in a primitive room without even her tote bag for company. No, that really wasn't like Peggy at all.

But what other explanation was there?

Noticing the gathering shadows in the room, she wondered how long she had slept. She glanced at her wrist to check the time, then remembered her watch was pinned to her bodice. She unfastened it, squinted at the dial, and received yet another unpleasant surprise. The expensive timepiece had stopped—probably when she hit the sundial. The face of the watch read six twenty-three.

Sighing, she slipped the watch onto her wrist and got out of bed. The rosebud-print dress she had removed was gone, and in its place, laid out neatly over the back of a chair, was a pretty yellow polished cotton one with a sweetheart neckline and pale lavender lace trim. She smiled when she saw it. Naturally, the actresses would have access to better costumes than the guests, which she supposed was one benefit of the new arrangement.

The dress was not a perfect fit—Abigail, as Amelia recalled, was fuller in the bust than she was—but it was close enough. She cursed the loss of her tote bag again when she couldn't find any bobby pins, but resigned herself to braiding her hair, doubling it up on the nape, and tying it with a yellow ribbon she took from a basket on the vanity table. After a moment she slipped the watch off her wrist and tucked it into the slitted pocket of her skirt. The watch was practically the only personal possession Amelia owned—at least until her bag was found. She was taking no chances with it.

She peered at her reflection in the mirror, but the room was too dark to see anything. She turned to find the light switch, knocked her shin on a blanket chest, and mumbled a curse as she hobbled over to the door.

She ran her hand along the wall on both sides of the door, following the wall all the way to the lamp at the bedside, but found no electric switch. She lifted the lamp from the table and found, to her amazement, that it had no electric cord. The base of the painted glass lamp was filled with oil.

She set the lamp down and tried not to give in to uneasiness. A room without a bathroom, she could understand; she didn't like it but it wasn't unheard of in old bed-and-breakfast inns across the country. But a room without electricity? Weren't there fire codes governing such things?

Part of the script, she reminded herself. *Just relax and enjoy it.* A weekend without indoor plumbing or electricity was not her idea of luxury accommodations by any means; but what was it Peggy had said— she had no sense of adventure?

Amelia supposed that for the sake of one weekend and a life that was badly in need of changing, she really should try to loosen up a little. If the other guests could put up with the inconvenience, so could she, and the least she could do was make an attempt to get into the spirit of things. But that didn't mean she had to leave her curiosity behind, and she couldn't help wondering exactly how far the production managers of this weekend's show were willing to go for the sake of authenticity.

She stepped out into the corridor and noticed that the gloom was dispelled by oil-burning wall sconces. She shook her head in bewilderment. Apparently there were no fire codes governing such things, after all, and she had to admit the soft, shadowy light did add an aura of mystery and romance. On impulse, she went to the door nearest hers and knocked softly. When there was no response, she twisted the porcelain knob and pushed open the door a crack.

This room was nothing like the green-sprigged one she had been assigned. It was smaller, it had only one bed, and there were shutters instead of lace curtains over the windows. She had been so certain all the rooms were decorated alike, which was how her own room had been switched without her noticing. But if that wasn't true . . .

Quickly, she closed the door and went to the next one. Feeling like a burglar, she repeated the procedure. That room had three small beds and showed signs of occupancy, with articles of clothing strewn about and a distinct scent of oiled leather, like boot polish, lingering in the air. It didn't look a thing like the room she had just left. And why didn't any of these people lock their doors?

By the time she reached the third door she didn't even bother to knock. Her heart was beating fast and her palms were damp and she blundered right in.

A masculine form in gray flannel trousers, a white shirt and suspenders looped over his hips was bending before the mirrored washstand, tying a string tie. She gasped, "Oh—I'm sorry!" and the man who'd been introduced as Jeffrey Craig turned toward her, looking not so much startled as curious.

Her cheeks burning, she started to back away, but he said, "Miss—Langston, is it?" He pulled the suspenders over his shoulders, scooped up his coat from the nearby chair and came toward her. "I'm glad to see you're recovered. Are you lost?"

"Yes. That is, I—" She thought quickly. "Actually, I was— I was looking for the ladies' room."

A faint, puzzled line appeared between his brows as he put on his jacket. "The what?"

"The bathroom. I know there's one on this floor. Don't let me bother you, I'll find it...."

Before she could escape, he stepped out into the hall with her, looking at her with a mixture of suspicion and indulgence that made her feel as though she would have done much better by telling him the truth.

Looking amused, he said, "You can't mean the water closet?"

After a moment, Amelia parroted, "Water closet?"

He touched her elbow lightly, turning her down the hallway. "I'll show you. It is a curiosity, I reckon. I've never seen anything like it. Professor Kane built it a few years back, but it doesn't get much use, I hear. Mother thinks it's unsanitary and Elliot says it wastes water. Personally, I think it's right clever. But then my opinion doesn't count for much around here anymore."

He opened a door at the end of the hall to a small room that contained an old-fashioned wooden toilet with a chain pull. "You're not going to ask me what it's for, are you?"

Amelia shook her head, relieved that at least there was some limit to how far they were carrying authenticity. She doubted whether many country homes had indoor toilet facilities in 1870, but an outhouse would have been more than she could have tolerated.

"You don't want to... er...?"

He paused delicately, and Amelia gave a nervous little laugh and shook her head. "No. But thank you for showing me. It *is* easy to get lost around here, isn't it?'' Quickly she turned toward the stairs again. ''Do you know where they're serving supper?''

''Having dined there with some regularity for most of my life, I think I can safely say the dining room. Would you allow me to escort you?''

He offered her his arm, which she took hesitantly. Old-fashioned manners were almost as hard to get used to as the script itself. But remembering her resolution to at least *try* to have fun, she decided to put her anxiety about the mix-up in the rooms aside for now.

She said as they walked toward the stairs, ''Who is Professor Kane?''

''Well, now, that is an interesting story, and not one I'm sure I can tell between here and the supper table.'' He had a pleasing voice, low and smooth with a drawl that was more of the West than the deep South. Some women were attracted to eyes, or smiles, or hands; for her, it was voices. And she liked Jeff Craig's voice. ''He's a crazy old geezer. Been around almost as long as I can remember and I don't know what for. Nobody does. But everybody likes him, so he stays. Now, why don't you tell me about yourself?''

Amelia was a little taken aback by the abruptness of the question, for she still wasn't sure exactly what role she was supposed to be playing. She gave a rueful shake of her head and replied, ''That might not be as easy as it sounds. Could you tell me about the other people here? Or would that be against the rules?'' It couldn't hurt, she reasoned, to get a head start on the mystery—especially since she had missed the opening party. And who knew? With a little help, she might discover she had an inborn talent for sleuthing, and surprise everyone.

Jeffrey Craig flashed her a puzzled look and replied, "No, it's not against the rules. There's my brother Elliot, who runs the plantation now, and my youngest brother Benjamin, who's getting ready to go away to the university in the fall. Dr. and Mrs. Calvert are visiting from Baltimore, along with Dr. Calvert's son by his first wife—Sam. And there's Colonel Talbot, an old friend of my father's, and Professor Kane. You'll meet them all in a moment. None of them bite, I assure you. Is there anything else you'd like to know?"

Amelia laughed. "Is that ever a leading question!" Starting with why her room was changed—and how— all the way up to what had happened to Peggy and her tote bag, Amelia had a list of things she would like to know that would keep someone explaining far into the night. But this man was not the one to ask, and she doubted he would tell her even if he knew. There was nothing to do but play the game.

So she shook her head and added lightly, "But I guess I'll have to find my own answers, just like everyone else."

Jeffrey murmured, "I guess you will." But she had the strangest feeling he wasn't talking about the solution to the mystery.

The others were gathered in a big, airy parlor off the main foyer, and Martha Craig rushed forward with her hands extended when Amelia and Jeff entered. "Jeff, dear, we were just about to go in. And I see you've brought our guest. Are you feeling much better, child? You didn't have to come down, you know. We would have sent a tray up." She took Amelia's hands and, without giving her a chance to reply, pulled her forward. "Come, let me make you known to everyone."

Amelia tried to put faces to the names Jeff had given her, knowing she wouldn't have a chance of solving the mystery if she couldn't remember the players. Elliot Craig bore a striking resemblance to Jeffrey; one could almost be convinced they were really brothers except that Elliot's good looks were shallower and more cultivated; he lacked the raw virility that Jeffrey displayed so well. Benjamin was young and slim with a teenager's awkwardness; if he hadn't been so young, Amelia might have suspected him to be one of the invited guests rather than an actor. Colonel Talbot was a big, square, blustery man with thinning red hair and an exaggerated Southern drawl. Amelia was almost sure he wasn't an actor. Dr. Calvert was small and quiet and stayed well in the background, but his wife looked like a thoroughly unpleasant person. She was big-bosomed and loose-jowled, with a loud voice and poor grammar. On her neck she wore a magnificent replica of the diamond-and-ruby necklace. It must have contained thirty-five karats' worth of stones and if it was anything like the real thing, Amelia could well imagine why someone would be tempted to steal it. Professor Kane, whom Jeff had described as "a crazy old geezer," seemed perfectly normal to Amelia except for his costume, which was a mismatched arrangement of brown twill trousers, a faded red shirt, and a yellow coat that was buttoned crookedly. His head was balding and dotted with liver spots, his jaw bristly and his expression a little vague, but there was nothing forbidding about him. He looked, as a matter of fact, like the only one in the room who was at ease.

Amelia didn't see anyone she recognized, although she hadn't really looked very closely at the people who were in the foyer when she'd checked in. One of them might be playing Colonel Talbot or Dr. Calvert, but she was certain she had never seen Mrs. Calvert before. And where was Karen? Where, for that matter, was Peggy?

She had no chance to ask those questions, however, as Martha Craig whisked everyone into the dining room. Amelia had never been comfortable in social situations where she didn't know anyone. With the added pressure of trying to act out a role, she expected the supper to be an endurance test, at the very least. In fact it was the opposite. The actors were so convincing, so involved in playing their parts, that she was hardly required to participate at all. In a short time she relaxed, enjoying the experience of what was, to all intents and purposes, a nineteenth-century family dinner.

Admittedly the food was delicious—it was probably one of the most authentically prepared representations of Chesapeake Bay-style cooking she had ever had.

"The meal is really wonderful, isn't it?" she commented to Professor Kane, who was seated to the right of her.

He looked at her sharply. "Do I know you?"

Startled, Amelia replied, "Well, no. I mean, I'm Amelia Langston."

"You from around here?"

Amelia fingered her necklace nervously and wished she had kept silent. "No, not really. I—"

"I don't know you," he announced, and returned to his meal.

Amelia wondered if he was supposed to behave so eccentrically. Or was that the way he was naturally?

Benjamin Craig, on her left, had noticed the exchange and smiled apologetically. "He's a little strange," he said softly, "but nice when you get to know him." Then, raising his voice a little and leaning forward, he said, "Say, Professor, do you think men will ever go to the moon?"

With his mouth half full of corn bread and without looking up, the professor replied, "Think they're already there. Think they're building cities up there right now, and looking down at us with big telescopes while we're having supper."

Benjamin shrugged and smiled at Amelia as though to say, "I told you so."

Mrs. Calvert tittered at the conversation, and the two Craig women looked embarrassed. Abigail, obviously looking for a way to change the subject, noticed Amelia toying with her necklace and exclaimed, "Oh, what a pretty trinket! Mama, did you see her necklace?"

"Why, it is lovely, my dear," said Martha Craig gratefully. "I don't believe I've ever seen anything like it. What is that design?"

"It's my initial." Amelia put her hand back in her lap. "An *A*."

"Well, isn't that clever?"

"My mother gave it to me for my birthday." By that time she was feeling comfortable enough to participate in the play. "It's nothing compared to Mrs. Calvert's, of course."

Mrs. Calvert obligingly lifted her thick jowls to show off the jewels, but no one looked. In fact, there was an obvious tension around the table as everyone seemed to deliberately avoid looking at Mrs. Calvert.

And then Colonel Talbot spoke loudly into the silence. "It seems some folks don't mind where they parade their fancy geegaws...or where they came from, either."

Mrs. Calvert made an indignant sound, and Martha Craig cast a pleading glance toward the colonel. Sam Calvert's fist tightened beside his plate. "Just what do you mean by that, sir?" he demanded.

"I mean, *sir*—" the colonel spat out the word as though it were a curse "—that there's not a God-fearing, law-abiding man or woman in this state that doesn't know how your kind fattened its purse—"

Dr. Calvert angrily interrupted, "I resent that, sir!"

Colonel Talbot turned on him. "And I resent the fact that yellow-blooded cowards are allowed to sit down at the table with good Confederates—"

Sam Calvert lurched to his feet, his face flushed. "Who are you calling a coward, sir?"

"I'm calling you a coward, and I'll call you a lot worse—"

"Gentlemen, please!" Elliot Craig's voice cut through the furor with icy calm. "Let's remember our place, shall we?"

Furious, the colonel turned to Elliot. "You can't mean to tell me—"

"I'm telling you," replied Elliot forcefully, "that this gentleman is a guest in my home. As are you. And I will have peace at my table."

For a long moment the two men locked stares. Finally the colonel turned away. He looked at Martha Craig, who appeared close to tears. "My apologies, ma'am," he said gently. And to Sam Calvert, he added more stiffly, "Sir, I forgot myself. This fine lady's table is no place for raised voices."

After a moment, Sam Calvert resumed his seat, his jaw muscles tense. But he wasn't willing to let it go. "I'm as good a Confederate as any of you," he muttered. "Just because I didn't fight..." He gave Elliot an accusing look. "You didn't fight, either. I don't see what you've got to be so high-and-mighty about."

Elliot didn't raise his eyes form his knife and fork but continued to cut his ham into small pieces. He said, "My brother was a hero to the Cause."

Jeffrey laughed softly. The sound was so inappropriate in the tension-filled room that it was startling. "So now I'm a hero, am I?" His eyes glinted as he looked at Elliot, and he appeared to be genuinely amused. "Is that your way of saying, 'Welcome home'?"

Elliot's color rose, but it was Mrs. Calvert who spoke. Her voice was high and nasal, and Amelia realized for the first time that she was the only one who wasn't affecting a Southern accent. "Hero, is it?" she asked. "So *that's* what they're calling it now."

Every man at the table stiffened, and Martha Craig made a small, stifled sound in her throat. Mrs. Calvert turned to her defensively. "Well, I'm sorry, Martha, but I've got just as much right to speak my mind as anybody here, and we all know what he is.''

Then Jeff defused the situation by smoothly agreeing, ''I don't think anyone would argue with that, ma'am. But before you start running down a list of my sins, this looks to me like as good a time as any to excuse myself.'' He dropped his napkin on the table and rose gracefully. ''Mother, a delightful meal as always. Ladies.'' With a general bow to the table, he departed.

A full three seconds' silence followed the sound of his last footstep. Then Martha Craig forced a smile and said, ''Well. We have a nice pecan pie and some apple tart left from dinner. Who would like iced coffee?''

Amelia felt like applauding. She was so wrapped up in the drama, so totally convinced by the performers, that it wasn't until Martha spoke that she fully realized it *had* been a performance. There were so many plots and subplots going on that she was getting dizzy trying to keep up with them. Yet at the same time she was thrilled. Peggy had been right. This *could* be fun.

The remainder of the meal was anticlimactic. Elliot tried to make conversation with her, but she found she really didn't like him much. He seemed miscast as a strong head-of-the-household, and came across as a weak man who was struggling to maintain authority he hadn't earned. Jeffrey would have been much better in the part.

When Martha Craig suggested the ladies excuse themselves and leave the gentlemen to their brandy and cigars, Amelia was relieved, but she found that being banished to a small parlor with the women was even more work than making conversation with Elliot Craig had been. Everyone had a piece of sewing to do except Amelia, and she felt like sitting on her hands. Abigail and Martha tried to draw Amelia into the conversation, while Mrs. Calvert watched her with narrow, buzzardlike eyes, as though waiting for her to make a mistake. It was exhausting, creating a biography in response to their questions. At last, making a comment about the warmth of the room, Amelia excused herself to step out onto the veranda.

Moving away from the window until she could no longer hear the other women's voices coming from the room, Amelia followed the curve of the wraparound porch to the darkened side of the house. *What a day!* True, dinner had been wonderful and the entertainment superb, but she was still ill at ease with these strangers and anxious about Peggy. Besides, there was a limit to how much adventure she could stand. She wished she were at home in her own bed.

If she were at home right now, she would pour herself a glass of wine, put on the sound track to *Les Misérables* and spend a thoroughly enjoyable hour and a half, laughing and crying along with the familiar music. At eleven o'clock she would watch a rerun of "M*A*S*H," shower and go to bed. That was her idea of a perfect evening.

And then she would spend the next two hours tossing and turning, wondering what she had done wrong with Bob, wondering what she was going to do about a job when her severance pay ran out, and wishing everything could be the way it used to be, because even though her life hadn't been great, at least it had been familiar.

And that was exactly, she firmly reminded herself, why this weekend was going to be good for her. Whatever else could be said for the mystery weekend, she hadn't thought of Bob or her state of unemployment once since arriving here.

The porch was very dark, although the sky was filled with stars. The air was balmy and richly scented with a variety of herbs and grasses, and the only sound was the chorus of crickets and tree frogs. It was rather charming and peaceful.

She smelled cigar smoke before she actually saw the man smoking. He was leaning back in a rocking chair on the corner of the porch, one foot propped up on the railing, the rest of his body deep in shadow. She was almost upon him when he swung his foot to the floor and stood, surprising her.

"Oh!" she exclaimed. "I didn't know anyone else was out here."

Jeff Craig stepped out of the darkness, a half smile curving his lips. "Since no one else knows I'm out here, either, I think your reputation will be safe."

Amelia hesitated, considering whether to go back the way she had come or to continue her stroll on the veranda. He was blocking the way forward. It seemed rude to just walk away, so after a moment she went over to the rail and looked out over the lawn. "It's nice here, isn't it?" she said.

He came closer. She realized then that what he was smoking wasn't a common cigar—the smoke was milder, the shape thinner. It resembled one of those combination cigar-cigarettes that showed up on old Westerns.

He took a final draw on the cigar and tossed it over the railing. Then he turned to her and asked pleasantly, "Who are you?"

Amelia blinked, startled. "What do you mean?"

"I mean, my dear Miss Langston—if that is your name—you are not Charlotte Landston's daughter from Charleston. You didn't arrive on the ferry this morning and you didn't lose your bags and you didn't just happen to stumble into the garden and swoon. So who are you?"

Amelia was relieved to abandon her role. "Right." She smiled. "My mother's name is Joanne and she sells real estate in Virginia Beach. I'm from Richmond, though I was born in Norfolk. As a matter of fact, I *did* lose my luggage, but I didn't even know there was a ferry. We came in over the causeway."

A deep frown-line appeared between his eyes. "Who is 'we'?"

"My friend Peggy. She's blond, about so tall—" she lifted her hand an inch or two above her head "—brown eyes. Maybe you've seen her."

The frown persisted. "There's no one like that here."

Amelia started to protest, then bit her lip. "I guess she really did leave," she murmured unhappily.

"So, you're by yourself?" There was an edge to his tone that puzzled Amelia.

"It looks that way," she answered.

"What are you doing here?"

Amelia shrugged. "I write a food column for a regional magazine—or at least I used to."

He looked at her, waiting for her to finish. When she had nothing more to add, the line between his dark brows deepened. He repeated, "Food column? Do you mean receipts and such?"

It took Amelia a moment to remember that *receipts* was a word used interchangeably with *recipes* in the deep South. She answered, "Well, yes, sort of. And I review restaurants and tell where the best places to eat are when you're traveling. That kind of thing."

His scrutiny was intense now. "And you do this for a living?"

She laughed a little. "Well, more or less."

"I see." He shifted so that his back was against the rail, and continued to look at her. "That's the most convincing thing you've said all evening."

"I beg your pardon?"

His expression was thoughtful. "You are a very unusual young lady. I don't know quite what to make of you."

Amelia had never been called unusual before, and wasn't quite sure whether to take that as a compliment. But there was something exciting, even romantic, about standing on the dark veranda with a handsome stranger. She had been part of a couple for so long that she had almost forgotten how to behave as a single woman and had dreaded the awkwardness of the dating scene. Yet with Jeff she felt no awkwardness—probably because of the element of fantasy involved.

She smiled and gave a self-deprecatory twist of her wrist. "There's nothing unusual about me. I'm as ordinary as dust."

"Is that right?" Even in the darkness, she could see amusement in his eyes. "You appear out of nowhere to swoon in the garden. You keep talking about this nonexistent friend of yours and luggage that I doubt very much you ever had. You look like a demure young Southern belle, but you say you work for a living as if you're proud of it. When my mother tried to make you drink buttermilk and wrap you in cold towels you fought like a panther—which is something no well-brought-up young lady would ever do. And you didn't blush when I showed you Professor Kane's water closet. No. I wouldn't say you're ordinary in the least. In fact, you're quite unlike any other woman I've ever known."

His statements confused her, and Amelia didn't know how to react. He didn't *sound* as though he were playing Jeffrey Craig now. She was becoming uneasy again, and looked away. The only response she could think of was, "You must have known some pretty strange women."

"I thought I had," he agreed easily, "until now."

Anxious to move the conversation along, she asked, "Tell me about yourself. What do you do when you're not doing this?"

Jeff surprised her by chuckling softly and said wryly, "Rob banks and trains, mostly—to hear people tell."

Amelia felt a surge of disorientation again, as though she were just a step out of time. The line between reality and fantasy was so blurred that she couldn't distinguish one from the other. Who had she been talking to all this time in the darkness: a handsome actor taking a break from his role, or the *real* Jeffrey Craig? The speculation sent a shiver down her spine.

Amelia shook her head—she was definitely getting carried away. "I thought you were a war hero," she countered, determined to stick to the scenario.

Jeffrey reached into his pocket and withdrew another cigar, looking at it for a long moment before he replied, "There were no heroes in that war."

His voice was low and tight with remembrance, and without thinking, Amelia nodded understandingly. "Just like Vietnam," she stated softly.

He looked at her. "Where?"

That caught her off guard. It was a little thing, and there had been much more glaring inconsistencies throughout the day. But the look in his eyes was the unfeigned bafflement of a man who had never heard of Vietnam, and it sliced through her like a knife. An irrational little voice insisted, *He's serious. This is no act. None of it has been an act—from the very beginning. This—*

But she cut the thought off, almost desperately, and quickly looked away. She swallowed hard, and when she spoke her voice was deliberately light. "So, do you really rob banks and trains?"

Jeff glanced at the cigar, then smoothly put it back into his pocket. "No, I don't. But I doubt if I could convince the federal marshals of that, if they ever caught up with me. I can't even convince my own family."

"And so—" Amelia said, her voice sounding breathless and false "—the plot thickens."

He murmured, "So it does. And I wonder just how much you have to do with that."

Surprised, she looked at him. "Me?"

His smile was grim. "It wouldn't be the first time women have been used as spies."

"A spy? Is *that* what I'm supposed to be?" Amelia vigorously shook her head. "Oh, no. Thank you very much, but I will not be a spy. It's too hard, and I'm not a professional. Let someone else be the spy. All I want to do is just sit back and watch."

He looked at her for two seconds in absolute silence. Then he laughed—a rich, full laugh. "No," he admitted, "you would never make a spy. But still ..." He cocked his head. There seemed to be more curiosity than accusation in his eyes now. "I can't help wondering what you are."

Amelia smiled enigmatically. "Maybe it doesn't matter. I mean, that's the whole point of this place, isn't it? To just let go of all the baggage of the modern world and escape into fantasy?"

After a moment, he returned her smile. "I feel that way about the island, too. I reckon that's why I keep coming back."

"To play the same role?" she teased him.

"Oh, no," he assured her. His eyes twinkled. "A different role every time. Sometimes the rebellious young man, sometimes the sober older brother, the dutiful son, the troublemaker ... and now the renegade outlaw on the run. What role are you playing, Amelia Langston?"

"Oh, I don't know." Amelia tilted her head back. There *was* a kind of magic about this place: the chirping of the night life, the stillness of the landscape. It was easy—perhaps too easy—to let her uncertainty and apprehension slip away, and to allow the fantasy to take over. It had been a long time since she had flirted, and she was thoroughly enjoying it.

"I don't think the role of demure Southern belle fits me—" she glanced at him sideways "—as you already pointed out. Maybe I'll be the homely poor relation who, by virtue of her modesty and goodness, wins the heart of the dashing prince—or, in this case, the plantation master."

"You're not suited for that role, either," he pointed out. "You're much too lovely to be a homely poor relation."

A flush of pleasure warmed her cheeks. She gave a light laugh and declared in an exaggerated Southern drawl, "Oh, sir, how you do run on!"

He smiled and lifted his hand, brushing a curl away from Amelia's face. The feather-light caress made her skin tingle, and the glow in his eyes was something she hadn't experienced from a man in a long time; it was exciting, full of promise.

"Besides," he said, "I don't think you'd like Elliot. He can be rather stuffy at times, and is not much given to playing games."

She responded, a little breathlessly, "Who said I was talking about Elliot?"

The boldness of her words astonished her, but then what did it matter? She was caught up in the fantasy and it was so easy, so wonderfully easy, to just let everything else slide away. This was what she needed—to put reason aside for a moment, to forget who she was and what was left behind in the real world; to pretend, just for a little while, that she was someone she was not.

Her pulse quickened and her breath grew shallow as he gazed down at her, so very intently. His scent was of crisp fresh cotton and leather, with the faintest hint of cigar smoke—masculine and richly evocative. He lifted his hand again, lightly tracing the curve of her neck with the backs of his fingers. The touch sent another shiver down her spine.

She said, "Maybe the role I play should be brazen hussy."

His lips curved in a smile that was teasing...and tender. "Or gentle seductress."

His hand closed upon her shoulder, gently kneading. His other hand slipped around her waist. She didn't resist as he drew her close.

His mouth covered hers and she was shocked at her reaction. This was no soft, exploratory kiss of a playful lover, no experimental tasting and clasping of a slow seduction. It was powerful, certain, unrestrained. His hands were hard against her back, his arms engulfed her, and his kiss went through her in a rush of searing heat, leaving her senseless, weak, melting into him. It was as if she had never been held by a man until he held her; as if she had never been kissed by a man until he kissed her. She felt, in that moment, as though she had never known any man before.

His mouth left hers but her head was still spinning, her body still throbbing. She clung to him. She couldn't get her breath. He touched her cheek with his lips and as hot as her skin was, his breath sent a new rush of fire through her. His hand slid up her back and tightened on her neck. He made to pull her close again, and her heart was going wild. Suddenly it didn't seem like a game anymore.

"No," she whispered. She never knew how she had gathered the strength to say that, nor to push her hand, however unconvincingly, against his chest.

The pressure of his hand lightened against her neck. His breathing was uneven, and yet his voice sounded almost normal as he murmured, "My dear Miss Langston, can I have mistaken you?"

She wanted to smile. She was sure he intended for her to smile. But the best she could do was to turn her head against his shoulder and say, "My...goodness."

His lips touched her hair. "I'd rather not talk about your goodness just now."

With all the willpower she had, she braced her hands against his chest and stepped away. His hands drifted slowly down and looped around her waist, holding her, yet not holding her. Her face was flushed and his eyes were dark with passion, but his smile was teasing. He asked, "Is something wrong?"

"Yes— No. I mean, I—I never intended..." Now she *did* feel like a simpering Southern belle and she stared at him helplessly. "I don't even know your real name!" she blurted, miserable with embarrassment.

His smile softened. With tender indulgence he said, "As it happens, my name is Jeff. I thought I'd told you. Do you have a real name?"

She swallowed, trying to make her voice sound calm. "Amelia. People call me—Amy."

His hand tightened, almost imperceptibly, on her waist. "And now that we've got that out of the way, do you feel better?"

She nodded, then shook her head. "I—I don't usually... I don't mean to be a flirt. I'm sorry."

"No." His voice was serious now, and he stroked her hair gently. Then he stepped away. "It's I who should apologize. I've been too long away from civilized company, I'm afraid. I've forgotten how to treat a lady." Gazing at her, he added softly, "And whatever else you are, you are a lady."

She searched his face, still confused as much by his behavior as her own. And she couldn't resist it. She had to say, "I've—never been kissed like that before."

He smiled. "That, I'm glad to hear. And it's been a long time since I've kissed lips as sweet as yours." His voice fell as he murmured, "Just once more?"

Before she could protest—though she had no thought of doing so—his lips clasped hers again, more gently this time, in a soft sweet tasting that lasted only a few seconds but seemed to go on forever.

He moved away. His eyes were on her lips as he said huskily, "Perhaps you'd best go in now. I haven't practiced being a gentleman in a long time.... It doesn't come easily to me."

She didn't want to go. Rather, she wanted to give in to the fantasy—to see how far it could go, to abandon herself for just one night to all that imagination had to offer. That would be foolish, of course, and she had no intention of following through. But never had temptation been so hard to resist.

After a moment she nodded her head and went inside.

* * *

Amelia lay awake for a long time in the four-poster bed. But it wasn't memories of Bob or anxiety about finding a job that made her restless—she just couldn't stop replaying the events of the day in her head.

Every time she thought about her behavior on the veranda her face flushed and her pulse raced. What had gotten into her? She wasn't the type of woman who fell into vacation romances. That was the kind of thing Peggy did. Was she really in such bad shape that she would allow herself to be swept off her feet by a good-looking stranger on a starlit night? She had always believed she had more self-control than that; and now she would have to spend the rest of the weekend avoiding him—except she really didn't want to avoid him.

But neither was she sure she wanted to stay the rest of the weekend.

Peggy would laugh. Peggy would say she was running away from her own fantasies. And maybe she was. Certainly she had gotten more than she bargained for with that one kiss on the porch, and she didn't want to examine too closely the feelings the encounter had stirred in her. If she did, she would have to acknowledge how much she had missed, all those years with Bob—all her life. Besides, Jeff Craig, or whoever he was, was—well, strange.

Everything here was strange. A lost tote bag, a missing roommate, a missing *room*. Antiquated plumbing and no electricity and actors who took their roles too seriously. Something was very wrong here....

She should leave. She wasn't having fun and the best thing to do would be to find someone to drive her to the beach resort in the morning, where she would no doubt find Peggy chuckling over a *mai tai* at the predicament she had left her friend in.

But what if she didn't find Peggy? Just how was she supposed to check into another hotel without any money or credit cards? Peggy could very easily show up tomorrow shaking her head in exasperation over what a wimp Amelia was. Since the whole trip had been Peggy's idea, shouldn't she at least give it a chance? At any rate, she couldn't do anything until she found her tote bag. And as much as she tried to tell herself to just relax and enjoy it, she did not like the feeling of being trapped.

She was just dozing off into a fitful sleep when a sound awakened her. Someone was strolling below, whistling a tune that was oddly familiar, and comforting. She fluffed up her pillow, closed her eyes, and let the melody lull her to sleep.

A few moments later she was wide-awake, listening hard for the whistling that was no longer there. But she had remembered the name of the tune, and took fierce, almost desperate reassurance from the first concrete reminder of the twentieth century she had experienced in hours. It was "Hey Jude," by the Beatles, and she lay back down with a smile on her face. Someone besides her, it appeared, had at last slipped out of his role.

FIVE

Amelia woke at dawn. Squinting in the light filtering through the lace curtains, she watched Abigail grip the bedpost while Lotti drew the strings of her corset tight, all the while thinking, *It's a dream. It has to be!*

Then the black woman said, "It's gonna be hot today, Miss Abigail. Hotter than yesterday. You want to wear that pretty blue muslin I hemmed up for you last night?"

"Hush, Lotti, not so loud," Abigail whispered. "Our guest is sleeping. Yes, the muslin will be fine."

"She's gonna miss breakfast if she don't get up out of that bed."

"She's not feeling well."

"Maybe I should fix her up a tonic."

Amelia lay with her eyes half closed and pretended to be asleep, but she was as wide-awake as she had ever been in her life. This was no dream. And those were not actors. At that moment, Amelia was convinced of it. No one went to that much trouble to put on a performance when there was no audience. No twentieth-century woman would allow herself to be trussed up in whalebone without at least a muffled curse when she thought no one was listening. No one could be *that* well-rehearsed, unless . . .

Unless something was going on here that was of far more significance than a mere "mystery weekend."

Her muscles were tense and her heart was beating far faster than it should have been this early in the morning. The brief pleasure she had enjoyed indulging in the fantasy last evening was forgotten as she made up her mind that she wasn't going to play along with this any longer. Something very strange was happening, and she was going to get to the bottom of it before another hour passed.

She sat up in bed and pushed aside the mosquito netting. "Good morning. Are you feeling any better?" Abigail asked.

"I feel fine," Amelia replied evenly.

Lotti bobbed a curtsy. "Morning, miss. I brought up your skirt for you. The grass stain came out real nice."

"Thank you."

Amelia watched as Lotti finished buttoning up Abigail's blue gown. "Now I understand why everyone had to have servants back then. A woman couldn't get into one of those costumes without one, could she?" she commented with an edge to her voice.

Abigail smiled uncertainly, and Amelia got out of bed, stretching.

"I think I'll just put on my regular clothes today, though. I don't suppose you found my bag?"

"No, not yet," Abigail replied soothingly. "But Mother has sent to the ferry to find out what—"

"I didn't cross on the ferry," Amelia said deliberately, turning to face her. "I'm not even sure there *is* a ferry. All my credit cards and money are in that bag, and I want it back. And while we're on the subject, why don't you tell me what happened to my room key and the clothes I wore in here—and my *room,* for that matter!''

Abigail cast a quick glance at the black woman and murmured, "That will be all, Lotti."

Lotti looked nervously at Amelia and then muttered, "Yes, ma'am." She hurried out the door.

When they were alone Amelia took a deep breath and said, as patiently as she could, "Look, I don't want to take this out on you. I know you're just part of the act. But I don't want to play anymore. If you'll just tell me where to find Karen I'll get this straightened out with her and be out of your way."

Abigail said, "Who's Karen?"

Amelia thrust her fingers through her hair and made a frustrated half-turn toward the window. "Oh, please!" Out of patience, she whirled on Abigail. "Look, there's no electricity in this room! There's not even a decent bathroom—and there were both when I checked in here yesterday afternoon! If this is the way you impress your guests, I've got to tell you this place will be out of business inside a month."

Abigail stammered, "I—I'm sorry you're not happy here—"

"I'm just not cut out for frontier living, okay? And I don't think this joke—or whatever it is—is very funny. And I'll tell you something else, which you can feel free to pass on to whoever is in charge. As far as I'm concerned, my things have been stolen, and none of you will think that's very funny if I don't get them back right now!"

Amelia saw the shock, mixed with no small amount of fear, spring into the other girl's eyes, and she couldn't believe she had said that. Amelia *never* made a scene. Usually, she was the kind of person who would politely swallow an inedible meal at a restaurant and still leave a generous tip; she would listen to annoying telephone calls from salesmen and as often as not buy something just to avoid being rude. She didn't even blow her horn in traffic. What had gotten into her, threatening a complete stranger over something that wasn't even her fault?

Amelia took an apologetic step toward Abigail. "Just tell me where Karen is," she said, more gently. "She's the one I need to talk to. *She'll* find my bag and I'll be out of here before you know it."

"I *can't* tell you where Karen is!" Abigail cried. Tears had sprung into her eyes. "I don't know who you're talking about!"

Amelia stared. The distress in the other girl's eyes was genuine, and when Amelia took another step forward Abigail backed away. That was not an actress's improvisation; there was genuine fear in her eyes.

Amelia said, as calmly as she could, "If you'll just stop this for one minute and tell me what you're trying to do..."

Abigail fumbled for the doorknob. Her hand was shaking. "You— You're not well—"

"Just tell me what's going on!" Amelia pleaded.

But Abigail had already fled, slamming the door behind her.

Amelia went over to the window and stared out. There had to be an explanation. A simple, reasonable, probably even harmless explanation. This was supposed to be a quiet little weekend with a group of overworked corporate types dressing up in costumes and playacting—the ultimate getaway vacation. And that was all it was, she reassured herself. It couldn't be anything else. Then why did she feel as though she had stumbled into a Hitchcock film?

She pushed her hair back with both hands, caught it at the nape, and nervously began winding it into a knot. *Okay,* she told herself. *Take it easy. You came here to solve a mystery, didn't you? Well, you've got one.*

But the truth was, she had never been very fond of mysteries, and she didn't think that attitude was likely to change just because she was the lead character.

Her gaze fell on the freshly washed and ironed rosebud-print outfit she had put on after she arrived yesterday, and, lacking a better alternative, she picked it up and began to dress. Even this simple act felt like a concession, almost an admission of defeat, and with every tiny button she fastened, her irritation grew. She wanted a bath. Her hair was frizzy and she needed her mousse and bobby pins. She wasn't even allowed the luxury of lipstick or mascara, and without it her face looked plain and washed-out—far too much like that of a character in a portrait from the days when even the most beautiful girls looked homely by twentieth-century standards. Not that it mattered, she assured herself. She wasn't here to compete in a beauty contest, and she had much more to worry about than her appearance.

She tried not to look at the paintings as she went down the stairs. She *could* have been mistaken about the portrait of Martha Craig. She hadn't really been paying attention at the time. There was no logical reason for someone to go to the trouble of rearranging paintings . . . just as there was no reason for a man of Jeffrey Craig's age and obvious education to pretend that he had never heard of Vietnam.

The "welcome" table in the foyer had been removed, as had the easel and directory announcing the day's events. The grandfather clock was there still, as were the clusters of brocaded love seats and chairs. She could smell coffee and country ham from another part of the house. But her appetite was—for once—the least of her concerns, and she went toward the front doors. She had given up on trying to reason with anyone inside the house. Outside, perhaps she could find a bellboy or a gardener or parking-lot attendant who could provide her with some information.

There was no one outside except Professor Kane. He was leaning back in one of the cane-seated rockers, thoughtfully contemplating a spider that was spinning its web between the eaves over his head and one of the columns. He didn't look around when Amelia came out, but she was sure he'd noticed her.

She said, "Good morning."

He grunted acknowledgement.

It seemed obvious that she wasn't going to get anything useful out of him, so she turned to go back inside. Then she noticed a folded newspaper on the floor beside his chair. "Is that today's paper?" she asked, picking it up.

"Yesterday's," he answered. "We're a day behind out here on the island.

Amelia unfolded the paper and noticed that it was a reproduction of a period publication—the Charleston *Gazette*. She was both impressed and mildly disgusted. These people didn't miss a trick.

She started to put the paper away and then she noticed the date. *June 14, 1870.* "They made a mistake on the date," she said.

With obvious reluctance, he dragged his attention away from the spider's web.

"Look." She pointed the date out to him. "That seems a little careless, don't you think? After going to so much trouble to get everything else right?" And she took cautious reassurance in the fact. Whoever was running this show wasn't perfect, and if they had made one mistake, they could make another. She didn't feel quite as trapped as she had a few moments ago.

Professor Kane said, without much apparent interest, "What day do you think it is?"

She thought a moment. "Yesterday was the third. Today's the fourth. Of July."

For a moment his mild blue gaze sharpened, then he seemed to lose interest again. He turned back to the spider's web. "Time's a funny thing," he mused. "All a matter of perspective. You take that spider there. Lives out his whole life in a matter of days. Since you came out here, a couple of years have passed for him. All a matter of perspective."

With a leisurely motion, he got up from his chair. "Guess I'll go on out to my workshop. Going to get some work done on my machine today."

Curious, Amelia asked, "What machine?"

"Perpetual motion," he replied, and started down the steps. "It's coming along fine, too. Just fine. You can come on out and watch if you want to. I don't mind."

A little dazed, Amelia watched him go down the stairs and around the corner of the house. Then she went back inside.

She methodically checked every room in the downstairs area of the house on her way to the dining room. Not one of them bore a sign saying Office: not one of them was a bathroom or a linen closet—two things she knew were absolute prerequisites in a hotel of any sort. Every room was decorated in period detail, and every room was empty.

Then she heard the voices from the dining room. The first one she thought belonged to Elliot Craig.

"For heaven's sake, Abigail, will you calm down? As if we didn't have enough trouble around here without you pitching a fit over having to share your room."

"But you didn't see her! You didn't hear the way she talked to me— The things she said! She's— There's something not right about her, Mother!"

Martha Craig said anxiously, "I thought the same thing yesterday, Elliot. Maybe we should have Dr. Calvert take a look at her."

"That old quack!" It was unmistakably Colonel Talbot's gruff voice. "He wouldn't know a dog bite from a bee sting, and if you ask me—"

Amelia couldn't listen to anymore. There was no way she could get past the dining room without being seen, but she didn't care. She picked up her skirts and ran.

She didn't know what she was running from—the humiliation of being talked about in such unflattering terms, her own indignation and frustration, or perhaps even the truth: The fact that once again the

actors had continued to perform without an audience
could mean nothing other than that *they were not actors.*

Amelia considered herself to be in good shape, but
as she ran the heavy skirts hampered her, the high humidity sucked away her breath, and her agitation
robbed her of strength. She had barely reached the
first big cypress at the start of the drive when she had
to stop, gasping.

She braced one hand against the tree. The only thing
that prevented her from letting out a string of curses
was that she didn't have the breath. She didn't hear the
footsteps behind her, nor did she know anyone was
near until she felt a firm touch on her shoulder.

She whirled around to see Jeffrey Craig standing
there, a broad-brimmed woman's hat in his hand. He
said mildly, "You forgot your hat," and offered it to
her.

She stared at him, still breathing raggedly, until,
with a lift of his shoulders, he set the hat on her head,
deftly tying the wide pink sash under her chin. It was
not a particularly intimate gesture. But his closeness,
the light brush of his fingers against her throat as he
tied the ribbon, brought back a rush of tingling sensations. The recent exercise was no longer entirely responsible for the flush in her cheeks or her erratic
breathing.

In the soft, morning light he was even more striking than he'd been last night. The cool green eyes were
alert and quietly penetrating. He wore his nineteenth-
century costume with a natural ease that enhanced,
rather than detracted from his masculinity. In fact,
standing beside him now in the full light of day, Ame-

lia could see what had so attracted her the night before—a subdued but unmistakable sexuality. Jeffrey Craig might be an act, but Jeff—whoever he was—was very real, very solid, and not so very different from the character he played. She only wished it was easier to tell where the actor left off and the man began.

She avoided his gaze and managed to regulate her breathing to a more normal rhythm. She said, after a moment, "This isn't my hat."

"No. It's my sister's." He didn't step away, and she felt him observing her. "You arrived without one, as I recall, and it's dangerous to be out in the heat without a hat."

The sun was hardly even above the horizon, and she noticed he wasn't wearing a hat of any kind. Still, it was thoughtful of him to follow her, and the unexpected gesture only confused her more. She nervously looked around the yard, but she couldn't avoid meeting his gaze forever. Abruptly she looked up at him and said, "Look, about last night... I don't want you to get the wrong impression. I don't usually do that sort of thing, and I don't want you to think I—"

"I assure you I would never think anything of the kind," he interrupted smoothly. Then he gave her a smile that was doubtless meant to be reassuring, but which only made her more uncomfortable. "Apparently you don't know much about men. We'll take any advantage that's offered us, but most of us know when to back away. That doesn't mean, of course—" he took her hand and tucked it securely through the crook of his arm "—that I won't try again. So consider yourself fairly warned."

Even as she shook her head, Amelia couldn't prevent an absurd tingle of satisfaction—even excitement—at his words. There must be prettier girls here this weekend, although, except for Abigail, she hadn't seen any of them; yet he had singled her out. That didn't happen to her often, which of course only made her more vulnerable. And she had to forcefully remind herself that the last thing she needed was to have her heart broken by a three-day fling with a resort-hotel Lothario.

He gestured toward the path ahead and she didn't try to retrieve her arm as she fell into step. But she did say, "I just want you to understand that I'm not interested in a weekend romance. Even if I was, I've got too many other things on my mind."

He murmured, "Yes, that's becoming obvious."

She talked too quickly and didn't bother to think about what she was saying, as she always did when she was nervous. "It's just that I really don't need this right now. I admit I got a little carried away, but I guess that's only natural after everything that's happened. The fact is, I just broke up with a man—or rather, he broke up with me—and I guess I'm not as recovered as I'd thought. The point is, I know it's your job to entertain the guests, but—"

He dropped her arm abruptly and turned to stare at her. On him, indignation took the form of icy anger. "Entertain the guests," he repeated. His voice was curt and the question sounded like a demand. "Is that what you think I'm doing?"

Immediately Amelia knew she had made a mistake. This man was no gigolo and that the thought could have crossed her mind was only another indication of her confusion. He might be an actor, and a very good one. He might enjoy teasing her and carry his role too far. But, looking into his eyes now, she was certain that seduction was not part of his job.

Plotting against her... The words echoed in her head with a touch of shame. But under the circumstances, wasn't a little bit of paranoia justified?

She said with chagrin, "I'm sorry. I didn't mean— I don't know what I meant. It's just that everything is so weird here and I don't understand any of it...." Suddenly she burst out, "Will you tell me what's going on? Do you *know?*"

Slowly his anger faded. Though she watched him closely, she could see neither the slightest flicker of hesitance in his eyes nor even a trace of duplicity on his face. His expression was thoughtful, and he replied simply, "No. I thought you could tell me."

Despair swept over Amelia. She turned on her heel, her skirts swaying behind her, and began to walk rapidly away. He kept step easily.

Amelia reached the door of a large, unpainted building, and after struggling with the latch for a moment, pushed it open. The interior was dark and dusty, filled with the sweet, musty odor of drying grains. There was nothing inside that didn't belong in a nineteenth-century barn, and she had somehow known that before she even looked.

"Someone's trying to gaslight me," she muttered, more to herself than him. "But who? And why?"

Determinedly she started walking again.

Jeff pulled the barn door closed, relatched it, and caught up with her in a few strides. "What are you looking for?" he asked politely.

"The garage. The only way to get here is by car. All those cars had to go somewhere. You can't hide a dozen cars."

She came to another building, and though it was far too small to hide a car she opened it anyway. It was an outhouse, and she closed the door quickly in disgust. Jeff stood by, looking amused.

She followed the circular pattern of buildings: a tall narrow smokehouse, a cool, mossy-smelling springhouse, a carriage house containing a coach and buggy. After each disappointment she walked faster and breathed harder until finally she reached the stable— her last hope, the *only* place that could be converted into a garage. But it smelled of hay and manure, and the stalls were filled with several riding horses and a couple of mules. There was a wagon with a broken wheel and a tack room filled with leather harnesses and saddles.

She walked back out into the sunlight, rubbing her aching temples. "There's got to be an explanation," she whispered. "There's *got* to be."

Her gaze moved over the fields, where the rows were dotted with figures bending and straightening to the rhythm of their hoes. Chickens clucked and squawked from their coop, and far away she heard the squealing of pigs in their pen. A peacock strutted by and a huddle of sheep grazed at the far end of the lawn. Woodsmoke rose from the chimney of the kitchen and a woman sang a soft, unfamiliar tune as she hung laundry on a line. It was all very rural and pastoral. And too, too real.

Someone was going to a great deal of trouble to convince her that she was actually living in 1870 with

the real Craig family. Not a reproduction, not a reenactment, but the real thing. Even the historic inns and
taverns of Williamsburg had exit signs and rest rooms.
Even Salem had streetlights. Even the Amish had
telephones . . . or at least had heard of them. But no
detail had been overlooked here, right down to the
actors who never once made a mistake.

She glanced at Jeff and then quickly away, trying to
suppress a shiver of dread. True, he wasn't as strange
as the rest of them, but when she reexamined every
minute of their time together, could she pinpoint a
single moment when she had been absolutely sure he
wasn't acting? A slew of wild theories went through
her head then, ranging from brainwashing to mass
hallucination to a CIA plot. Maybe she had dreamed
the whole thing. Maybe that blow on the head yesterday had been more serious than she thought. Maybe
she *was* living in 1870 and her memories of 1992 were
the dream.

She wished Captain Kirk were here. He would know
what to do.

At just that moment, Jeff said, "My sister thinks
you're quite mad, you know."

Amelia gave a choked laugh. At that same moment, she wasn't certain she disagreed. "And you
don't?"

"No," he replied. "I don't."

Feeling hopeful, she looked at him. He knew. Or he
must know . . . *something*. "Why not?" she asked
breathlessly.

His expression was thoughtful. "I'm not quite
sure," he said. "Perhaps I've been accused once too

often to make judgments upon others. Perhaps I've seen too much to doubt anything anymore."

He gave her a cynical half smile that mocked himself as much as her. "Then again, perhaps your madness is the very thing I find so appealing about you. This wouldn't be the first time I've taken up the banner for a lost cause, and I'm sure it won't be the last."

That response was disappointing, to say the least. Morosely, Amelia scanned the landscape once again, looking for something she had missed, racking her brain for some clue she had overlooked, some improbable theory she hadn't yet examined.

Her gaze fell upon the white house she had seen from the upstairs window yesterday. Had it been only yesterday? It seemed that years had passed between then and now, and she felt like Professor Kane's spider, spinning out the web of her life in a matter of days.

"What is that building?" she asked, pointing.

"That's the summerhouse." He took her arm again. "Would you like to see it?"

It seemed too small to house a fleet of automobiles, or anything else of significance, and she shook her head. He wouldn't have offered to take her if there had been anything to hide, and it was becoming clear that the answer to her mystery was not on the grounds around the main house.

She had a sudden thought. "Jeff, would you do something for me if I asked?"

He inclined his head gallantly. "Anything to be of service."

"Take me to the beach. I've got to find Peggy, and that's the only place she can be." But it was more than just a need to find Peggy that rose up with an urgency so intense it almost choked off her breath. She had to find *civilization*. Beach umbrellas and bikinis, poolside bars and paved parking lots, waiters in Hawaiian shirts and white shorts... Reality. And if she didn't find it soon, she really would lose her mind.

Jeff looked up at the sky. It was a habit he had, Amelia had noticed; something that was bred into farmers but one rarely noticed in city people—yet another example of how well-suited he was to his role.

He replied, "I don't see why not. We can get up there and back before it gets too hot. I'll go get Abigail."

"No!" She grabbed his arm. "I don't want her to come, and I don't have time to wait for her. Will you take me, please?"

"You're certain you want to go up there with me without a chaperon? Your mother wouldn't approve, you know. Neither would mine, if it comes to that."

"Oh, please!" She almost stamped her foot in impatience. "Can we just go? Now?"

He regarded her with skeptical amusement, then turned back to the stable and shouted, "Skinner! Hitch up the buggy, will you?"

Amelia released a breath of relief.

On that jolting trip Amelia discovered for herself just how far the human mind will go to convince itself to believe the unbelievable. In truth she had been doing exactly that since yesterday afternoon: ignoring signs, inventing excuses, pretending with all her might that everything was just as it should be until indications of the opposite practically exploded in her face. Even then, she assured herself there was a rational explanation and the fault was hers for not finding it.

As the buggy bounced over the dirt roads that took them away from the plantation, Amelia clung to the cushioned leather seat until her knuckles turned white and frantically rationalized away evidence of the fact that this was not the same Aury Island she had traversed only yesterday. They passed a village cluttered with wooden shacks she and Peggy must have missed on their tour yesterday, and marshlands planted with rice and workers in overalls and long calico skirts, thrashing the grain with tall staffs.... Well, most of the time she had been reading from the brochures. She hadn't seen everything. The junglelike growth seemed thicker than it had yesterday. But obviously Jeff was taking a different route to the beach. She and Peggy had driven on smooth blacktop pavement complete with stop signs and discreetly painted wooden street signs. *Hadn't they?*

The stillness of the soupy-hot morning was broken only by the buzz of insects and the creak of buggy springs, and after fifteen minutes of traveling the silence became more than Amelia's nerves could bear. She began to chatter.

"I guess you think I'm pretty silly. It's not that I'm a bad sport—at least usually I'm not—it's just that I don't like adventure very much. I really didn't want to come here in the first place. I knew it wasn't the kind of thing I'd enjoy. Peggy's always trying to get me to go white-water rafting or hiking in the Rockies or to take one of those helicopter tours of Alaska. And they always sound great, but for somebody else. Maybe I'm just lazy, but I don't see the point in paying to get stressed out on a vacation—I have enough challenges in my everyday life.''

He gave her a peculiar look but said nothing.

She was losing confidence with every moment. She continued to talk just to distract herself. ''I guess you're the type of man who enjoys outdoor sports.''

''I'm not sure I know what you mean.''

''Oh, hunting and shooting and camping out. That sort of thing.''

He chuckled. ''I'm not sure I'd call hunting a sport—not in the places I've been, anyway. As for camping, I'd as soon have a roof over my head and clean sheets to sleep on any day.''

She smiled nervously. ''Me, too. I hate bugs.''

That made him laugh.

After a time he pulled the buggy over to the side of the path and wound the reins around the brake. ''It will be easier to walk from here,'' he explained. ''You can see the ocean from over that rise.''

Amelia looked around uncertainly as he sprang down and walked around to assist her. ''Are you sure this is the right beach?''

''The island only faces the ocean on one side,'' he reminded her, and she knew that. She had seen it clearly on the map yesterday. But this was definitely not the approach she and Peggy had taken. Everything looked different. So abandoned and empty and...different.

There was a narrow sandy footpath leading upward through a thick growth of sea grass and twisted wild shrubs. It was a steep incline, and Jeff stayed a little behind her, his hand on her back as he guided her. Amelia cursed her long skirts as she tripped more than once, but Jeff was always there to steady her.

She could hear the call of sea gulls and taste the salty air. It was hot, and a sticky film of perspiration already clung to her face. A warm breeze caught the wide brim of her hat and flipped it backward. She heard the soothing lap of the surf just below. She hurried the last few steps.

They emerged on a long flat hilltop and Amelia had been so sure of what she would see that for a moment she almost *did* see—a wide white stretch of sand dotted with colorful beach umbrellas in front of discreetly arranged hotel buildings; bronzed bodies stretched out on beach towels; children splashing in the waves.

What she actually saw was an empty stretch of narrow, unkempt beach curving gently from horizon to horizon. The blue-green surf surged and receded, leaving corpses of driftwood and a treasure of shells in its wake. Sea gulls squawked and dived. But everything else was gone.

Completely gone.

SIX

Amelia didn't know how long she stood there, staring at the ragged, empty beach below, before the truth sank in. And even then, she wouldn't completely believe it.

At first she felt betrayed. It was a primal, gut-wrenching fury that made her want to fling herself down and beat her fists against the sand as though in retaliation. The resort wasn't *here*. All this time, the only thing that had anchored her to reality was the assurance that just across the island, just down a twisting turn of road, life went on as usual. People drank syrupy tropical drinks and wore saris and sunglasses and showered with little bars of soap shaped like seashells.... And Peggy was there. And telephones and automobiles and televisions were there. She had *counted* on it. But someone had robbed her of her last hope of salvation—civilization had been ripped away before her very eyes.

Then she thought, *We must be in the wrong place.* Frantically she turned to the left, to the right, and then around in a full circle, searching. An entire resort complex couldn't just disappear. They *must* be looking at the beach from the wrong angle. But the beginning and end of the beach were clearly defined in the same gentle curve she remembered from yesterday.

And then she noticed something else. There were no ships in the water. Amelia had never been to a beach in her life without catching at least a glimpse of a trawler, a shrimp boat, or an oil tanker. And something else. How long had it been since she'd heard an airplane overhead? The Charleston airport was less than seventy miles away, not to mention the naval air station, which was always testing along the coast.

And she remembered dozens of things, hundreds, pelting down upon her like sharp hailstones, pricking and cutting and leaving her icy cold. The ordinary sounds and sights and smells of modern life were gone—the hum of machinery, the muted swish of traffic on distant roads, telephone poles, yellow signs saying Buried Cable, fire hydrants, the smell of the insecticide that was used on swampy areas, highway signs, traffic lights, window screens . . .

She was shaking and couldn't catch her breath. She dared not think. . . .

She turned to Jeff. "What day is it?" she demanded hoarsely.

He wrinkled his brow. "I'm not sure. It's hard to keep up with days out here. The middle of June, I know that much. The fourteenth or fifteenth."

Exasperated, she screamed at him, *"What year?"*

Her hysteria was matched by an expression of shock on his face. But he quietly replied, "It's 1870."

She wanted to fling herself at him. She wanted to beat him with her fists and scream at him and call him the liar he was— But he wasn't lying. She knew it then as she should have known it before. She just couldn't believe it. She couldn't allow herself to believe it.

A cry rose up in her throat but was choked off by a wave of nausea. The seascape tilted and the sand beneath her feet was slippery and she felt herself swallowed up by horror. She saw the concern on Jeff's face as he instantly reached for her, but she flung out an arm to ward him off. She stumbled a few steps, then fell to her knees, overcome by a violent fit of retching.

She didn't know how long it went on. She was aware of Jeff kneeling beside her, holding her shoulders, stroking her hair away from her face, murmuring soothing words. And in the midst of it all, the one coherent thought she had was that she didn't want Jeff to see her like this, so she attempted to push him away. He stayed.

And when at last she was too weak to do anything but lean against him and choke back hiccuping sobs, he passed her a clean handkerchief and murmured, "It's all right. Let me get you into the shade."

With an arm around her waist he guided her gently to her feet, and somehow Amelia managed to take a deep breath. She said, "I—I'm all right. Some girls faint, or cry.... I throw up."

And then she looked up at him, fighting another wave of horror and disbelief. "My God," she whispered. "You really are Jeffrey Craig, aren't you?" Jeffrey Craig, who had lived and died over a hundred years ago, yet who stood beside her now, touching her, warm and strong and as solid as stone... He hadn't changed. She hadn't changed. It was *time* that had changed.

His face was grim as he said, "Come over here and sit down."

She was too weak to protest as he led her to the shade of a cypress and lowered her to the scrubby grass beneath. Her skin was clammy and she wasn't at all sure her legs would have supported her another minute.

He sat beside her, soberly watching her but making no attempt to converse or to question. Even then, it occurred to her what an extraordinary man he was, and she was grateful for his presence.

"The sundial," she said slowly. Her voice grew stronger as she thought back. "Everything was all right until I went into the garden… The storm… And all that electricity. It *could* have been— It must have been— Something happened. Some kind of time warp. Like a portal."

It made perfect sense. But did she honestly believe things like that were possible in the real world?

Or perhaps she had merely hit her head, and all this was a hallucination. Was it any more difficult to believe that she could hallucinate nineteenth-century corsets and farm implements and outhouses than to believe that she had traveled back in time? Did it matter?

Absently she ran her hand over her face—tears were streaming from her eyes, but she couldn't stop them. She looked at Jeff and tried to smile. It was more of a grimace, she suspected. "Maybe," she said thickly, "you'd like to reconsider what you said earlier about the state of my mental health."

His face was grave, his eyes penetrating. "I know something is wrong," he said. "I know you have problems, but I don't think dementia is at the root of them. That answer would be entirely too easy, and I suspect something more complicated is going on. Perhaps you could explain to me, the best way you can, what *you* think."

What Amelia wanted to do, more than anything else in the world, was just to lay her head against his chest and feel his strong arms around her. She wanted to close her eyes and let everything slip away. But she couldn't do that. She had to talk about it, she had to say the words, she had to have someone else hear them. Because talking about it, she knew instinctively, was the only thing that would ever cement her fragile hold on reality.

She looked down at the handkerchief he had given her, which was still clutched in her fist. She unfolded it, pressing out the wrinkles over her knees, then began to pleat it into narrow strips. She began, "Yesterday, Peggy and I drove here from Richmond. Actually, we took two days, and kind of toured the countryside and enjoyed the scenery...."

She was digressing. She paused to wipe the tears again. "This—this place—" she made a gesture toward the beach "—was a beach resort, with hotels and lounges and restaurants. The house—your house— was a hotel that was just opening, and the management had invited some complimentary guests in the travel and tourism business for a mystery weekend That's what we were doing here. The roads—" She gulped a breath, and tried to steady herself. "The roads were all blacktop, and the hotel had electricity, and Peggy took a shower in the bathroom in our room and used her curling iron, and the parking attendant took our car and a woman named Karen gave us maps and an information packet about the weekend. It was..."

She looked up at him helplessly, knowing what her next words would sound like to him. But she didn't know any other way to put it. "It was July third, 1992," she said.

His face remained expressionless. Waves broke in the distance and a sea gull cried out, but between them, the silence was absolute.

Amelia dropped her gaze. "I had trouble with my costume, and I was late for the welcome party. I got lost in the gardens, and a storm was brewing. There was something—something around the sundial, like a magnetic charge. It took the bobby pins right out of my hair and made my skin feel like it was on fire. I started to run, and I tripped and fell and when I woke up everything was different. When I woke up...it was 1870," she whispered.

Still silence. She didn't dare look at him. She stared instead at the pleated handkerchief in her lap, and after a moment she brought it to her face, blotting her cheeks, wiping her nose. She took a deep breath, steadying herself. She looked back toward the ocean but she didn't really see it. She was too numb to see or feel much of anything.

She said tiredly, "You think I'm crazy. I don't blame you. I've been thinking all of you are crazy since I met you yesterday afternoon."

After a long time, Jeff reached over and took her hand. The gesture startled her and she looked at him. His head was lowered, his eyes upon the hand he held so gently, so warmly in his. He said quietly, "Amelia, in my lifetime I have seen men blow each other apart for no other reason than the difference in the color of their coats. I've waded through fields of arms and legs and I've drunk from streams pink with blood and I've thought to myself, *This is insanity.* I've seen balls of fire race across the desert and consume a man alive, I've seen the earth open up and spew steam to the sky, I've seen whole towns buried by a sandstorm in a matter of minutes. I've seen, with my own eyes, a dead man brought back to life by an Indian medicine chief with a bag of rattles and bones. After a while, I stopped wondering what was sane and what wasn't.''

He looked at her. His eyes were dark and sober. ''Don't ask me to believe your story, Amelia,'' he said simply. ''Because I can't do that. But I can't say you're crazy, either.''

Slowly, Amelia moved into his arms, resting her cheek against his chest, closing her eyes, holding him. Being held by him. That, at the moment, was all she could ask for. And it was enough.

Without being asked, Jeff took a route toward home that followed the coastline, understanding that the only thing that would allow her to finally accept her newfound reality was the evidence of her own eyes. Any remaining doubts she had were erased completely on the journey home.

She asked dully, ''What do they do with crazy people in your century? Lock them in the attic?''

''Sometimes,'' replied Jeff equitably. ''Sometimes they're given over to the loving care of their families, which can be even worse.''

"My family," Amelia said slowly, "hasn't even been born yet." She tried to think about that, to absorb it and adjust to it, but she couldn't. It was simply too much.

She took a breath. "It's still possible," she continued bravely, "that I'm imagining all this. That when I hit my head . . ."

Jeff shook his head. "Any blow on the head that was hard enough to make you invent a story as wild as this," he told her bluntly, "would have killed you."

That made Amelia smile. "You have a strange way of reasoning."

"Coming from you, I take that as a compliment."

"Anyway, it doesn't make any difference, does it? I'd rather believe that this is really happening, impossible as it is, than believe I'm crazy. Of course," she added with a worried glance at him, "that doesn't help *you* decide what to think."

Jeff seemed perfectly at ease, and he kept his eyes on the narrow path. "Seems to me you have enough problems without worrying about what I think."

He was right, of course. But how could she not wonder about what he thought? He was the only other human being who shared her secret, and she wanted to know what he *thought.* Apparently Jeffrey Craig was not a man who was accustomed to sharing his private opinions lightly, and she supposed that under the circumstances she should be grateful for his silent acceptance of her.

"It's just that I'm the last person something like this should have happened to. It took me five years to adjust to the move from Norfolk to Richmond. How am I supposed to adjust to a whole new century? I depend on things being the same and staying the same. I've never been able to cope with change. The new fall television schedule throws my whole system off balance, for heaven's sake, and now there's not even such a thing as television—'' Her voice broke unexpectedly, and she blinked her eyes fiercely and clenched her fists. "I can't deal with this," she said definitely, fighting back panic. "I just can't deal with this."

"Of course you can," replied Jeff casually. He directed the horses into the tree-lined lane that led to the house. "You're better equipped to deal with this than any woman alive."

"How do you know?" she cried. "What do you know about any of it? You don't even believe me— you told me so yourself. And if you don't believe me, nobody will. So what am I supposed to *do?* Haven't you heard a word I've said? I don't belong here! My life is a hundred and twenty-two years in the future and I—''

Suddenly she gasped, struck by an idea so powerful that it literally took her breath away. "The sundial," she whispered. Hope made her giddy. "Of course!" she exclaimed. "It brought me here, it can send me back!"

Jeff looked at her blankly, and she grasped his arm urgently, her fingers digging into the fabric of his coat. "The sundial!" she insisted. "Don't you see? That's the way it always happens in science-fiction movies! Oh, Jeff, hurry! Please!"

She leaped out of the buggy almost before it had stopped moving. The train of her skirt caught on the buggy wheel, giving the shocked servants—and Jeffrey Craig—a quick view of her bare legs before she

impatiently snatched the material away. She caught up
her skirts in one hand and hurried toward the side of
the house.

"Which way?" she demanded breathlessly. "I
didn't come this way the first time. Where is the sundial?"

Jeff calmly touched her arm and gestured her to the
left.

She recognized very little of the landscape as she
followed Jeff's lead, winding through arbors and
shrub-lined paths. There were trees where she remembered no tree before, and no trees where there should
have been trees, and the shrubbery was all wrong. She
trusted Jeff to know his own garden, but with every
step they took she found it increasingly difficult to
hold on to the surge of hope that had sustained her.

Everything was different. The neglected, over-
grown garden was now a sunny patch of lawn planted
in ivy and bordered by shrub spruce. The huge tree
that only yesterday had completely hidden the house
didn't seem as tall. But the sundial was still there,
weathered with age, its granite contours impassive and
serene. The shadow across its face set the time near
eleven o'clock.

Amelia stood about ten yards away, breathing hard,
her heart racing. This had to be the answer. It *had* to
be. Because if it wasn't . . .

She didn't think about that. She couldn't.

She said hoarsely to Jeff, "You'd better stay here."

She started forward. Jeff, with a look of thoughtful amusement on his face, ignored her advice and
followed her.

She walked slowly, picking her way carefully over the thick carpet of ivy. With every step she expected the electricity, the winds, the peculiar magnetic effects to begin. She held her breath in anticipation of them; she stretched out her hands as though she could will a recreation of yesterday's events into place. The day remained sunny, the winds calm, the atmosphere placid. When she was only one step away from the sundial, hope was all but gone. Finally, almost prayerfully, she placed her hands upon the dial. All she felt was sun-warmed stone.

She stood there for a long time, her shoulders sagging, her head bowed. Jeff's voice roused her at last.

"That story you told Mother yesterday—about lightning and magnetism. Is this what you were talking about?"

She nodded, too defeated to even feel despair.

He said, "Odd."

Something about the tone of his voice made her look up. He was staring at the sundial, a frown bisecting his brow.

She roused enough energy to inquire, "What is it?"

For a moment he didn't answer. Then he shrugged, and looked at her. His tone was casual but the frown hadn't completely disappeared. "Nothing. I was just remembering something."

"What?" she demanded. Something faintly akin to hope stirred again.

He hesitated and then said, "The island is filled with legends. Most places like this are, I reckon. One of them is that this house was built on native holy ground. In fact, it wasn't until Great-Grandpa's time that anyone would even build up here—the old house used to be closer to the river. He got tired of fighting the snakes and gators, I guess—not to mention the floods—and built farther up. They'd been living here about ten years when my great-grandmother got the notion to put in a sundial—she was a Frenchwoman, you know, and I reckon things like that were popular over there. Anyhow, she had the gardeners clear out this patch here behind the house and they were setting up this thing—" he nodded toward the sundial "—when, so the story goes, one of the workers disappeared right before the others' eyes. They said the air just swallowed him up. It was years after that before they could even get servants to work in the house, and even now we can't get the gardeners to dig out here. That's why Mother just put down the ivy and let it go."

Amelia took a breath and released it shakily. Could that hapless gardener have been an unsuspecting victim of time travel, just as she had been? Should she feel better just because it had happened to someone else?

She asked, with difficulty, "What—happened to the gardener? The one who disappeared?"

"As far as I know, he never showed up."

Amelia looked at Jeff steadily. "Now do you believe me?" she demanded.

He replied, "I'm not sure what I believe." He started to turn away.

Furious, Amelia grabbed his arm. She wasn't angry with him, but she was angry—helpless and frustrated and overwhelmed by the enormity of it all—and his casual indifference was more than she could bear. She cried, "You've got to believe something! You can't just stand there and listen to a story like what I've just told you and nod your head and walk away! I need help here. Can't you see that? I need to know what you *think!*"

There was no sign on his face that he was moved at all. But his voice was a little rougher than usual, and beneath the material of his coat Amelia could feel his arm muscles tense. He said, "What do I think? Well, I have a couple of choices, don't I? The most obvious is that you are mad. Then again, maybe you're simply lying, making up this elaborate tale to get attention or divert attention from some even more desperate scheme. . . ."

With every word he spoke, Amelia felt her spirits sink deeper; her hand fell away from his arm. In those few moments, she felt more alone than she ever had in her life.

"And then there's the final possibility," he continued, and his eyes narrowed a little as he looked at her. "Which is that you're telling the truth. Maybe you do come from another century, and maybe in your time things like this are possible—even common. What do I know about the future? I've never thought about it. Thinking is a habit men get into when they have nothing better to do, and, frankly, just staying alive has always given me plenty better to do."

"Of course," she said softly, without looking at him. "Survival." Always the first order of business when the landing party found itself stranded on an alien planet. And in this century, survival was a matter of daily concern even for those who were born into it. She had better learn to adjust and do it quickly if she intended to fare as well.

Jeff's voice was gentle as he said, "I'm not the one to ask. I don't know what to think. But I'll give you a little free advice, if you want it."

She looked up at him slowly, reluctantly.

He said, "I wouldn't talk to any of the others about this if I were you. They're not likely to be as understanding as I am." A small twist of his lips followed that statement. "I guess that's because they've got a lot more to lose than I do."

Amelia thought back over the encounters she'd had with the other members of the family, seeing each episode from their point of view. A shudder went through her as she realized what they must think of her—and how dependent she was on the hospitality of these strangers. She had no place to go but here. If they decided she was mentally unbalanced—if they even found out she wasn't who they thought she was—what would happen to her?

She couldn't go home, not ever again. And there was no welcoming place for her in this century; no friends, no relatives, no one to whom she could turn if she got into trouble. She had to learn to adjust to survive, and she had to begin here.

She said tiredly, "I'm sorry I got you involved in this, Jeff. It isn't fair to expect you to understand, and this really isn't your problem. I should never have told you. I didn't mean to complicate your life."

The silence that followed was not what she expected, nor was the look in his eyes. His gaze was intense and probing, shadowed by sadness that seemed to carry with it a measure of frustrated helplessness. She knew then more clearly than she ever had before just how impossible a story she had asked his nineteenth-century mind to accept, and how deep a struggle he must be undergoing. How much more could she ask of him? Wasn't his mere silence after all that had happened a sign of extraordinary heroism?

Then he smiled and shook his head. "You didn't involve me," he said. "I was involved from the moment I came upon you crumpled in the garden. I told you, didn't I, that I have a notorious weakness for lost causes?"

He extended his arm to her and, after a moment, Amelia accepted it, smiling hesitantly. Together they walked back to the house.

SEVEN

Amelia passed the remainder of the day in a haze. Dinner, the largest meal of the day, was served at noon, but she barely remembered what she ate. Afterward, she learned, it was the custom for the ladies of the house to "lie down for a while"—a practice she would come to appreciate through the hot summer afternoons that followed, but on that day she was grateful merely for the opportunity to be alone with her thoughts.

She made a point to be very careful about her behavior around the others and even apologized to Abigail, privately and sincerely, for the way she had acted earlier in the day. Though Abigail was obviously too well-mannered to allow her skepticism to show, Amelia had a feeling the girl wasn't as gullible as she appeared. It would take some work to make a friend of Abigail Craig.

When she thought of friends—the ones she'd left behind, the ones she could never hope to find in a century in which she had nothing in common with anyone—the first tears slipped down her cheeks, and once they started she couldn't stop them. Lying in that hot room with Abigail napping peacefully on the bed next to hers, Amelia stared at the ceiling through the gauze of mosquito netting and she cried for her mother, who would never know what became of her daughter; her sisters, whom she kept meaning to call but never seemed to get around to it; for the work she had sometimes hated and sometimes loved and would never do again; for Peggy and for Joyce who lived next door and for the girls she had gone to school with and was still close with, and for all those familiar faces that had seemed like such a minor part of her life until she knew she would never, ever see them again.

She cried for *Star Trek* and electric hair-driers and the sound of ringing telephones and the car she hadn't even finished making payments on. She cried out of anger and frustration at the unfairness of it all; she indulged in a good healthy fit of self-pity. She owed herself that much. And when her chest was aching from sobbing and her face was hot and itchy from the scalding tears and she was too tired to weep anymore, she stared up at the ceiling again and tried to make some plans.

Planning was one of Amelia's strongest talents. She planned her route to the grocery store. She planned events in her day. She even made lists of what she was going to say on telephone calls. A trip such as the one she and Peggy had taken to Aury Island required weeks of poring over maps, tourist brochures and travel magazines. Bob used to accuse her of taking all the spontaneity out of life; and she supposed that was true. She planned to avoid surprises and to avoid dealing with the unexpected and had honed the skill to a fine art. But how could she make plans when she didn't even know where to begin?

One of the most important things she had to do was to make friends with Martha Craig and her family. This was not motivated purely by selfish needs; she would have done the same even if theirs was not the only household in this century that could offer her food, shelter—and a chance to start over. They were her hosts, and things hadn't changed that much in a hundred years. Although she hadn't proved it to this point, Amelia did know how to be a good house-guest.

She was surprised at how little effort was required on her part to ingratiate herself with her hosts who, living in an era when Southern hospitality was more than just a concept, were more than happy to accommodate. She admired a piece of cross-stitching that Abigail was working on and asked her to teach her the art. Though obviously astonished that Amelia had never acquired such a basic skill, Abigail was flattered and promised to draw out a pattern for her that evening. In the late afternoon, she found Benjamin on the veranda and offered to play a game of checkers with him. He was a charming and entertaining companion and she enjoyed the game tremendously—even though she did sacrifice her competitive streak to the conventions of the time and allowed him to win.

At supper she complimented Martha Craig with absolute sincerity on the succulent batter-fried fish, and the other woman beamed. When she offered to allow Amelia to look at her recipe book, which was the most treasured secret of any household of the time, Amelia knew she had scored a major triumph.

In comparison to the previous evening, supper was a quiet affair. Mrs. Calvert was no more irritating than was her apparent nature, the gentlemen were well-mannered, and there was a great deal of talk about the rain that hovered oppressively in the air but never broke. Amelia concentrated on the impression she was trying to make—and on watching Jeff, listening to Jeff, waiting for him to do something or say something that would reveal the secret they shared. He never did, and she supposed she should be grateful for that.

Although it was only the second time she had seen him with his family, Amelia couldn't help noticing that he was a different person with them than he had been alone with her. He answered politely when spoken to but made no other effort to contribute to the conversation, and the only people who ever spoke to him were his mother and Colonel Talbot. Everyone else seemed ill at ease around him; and it was as if Jeff, sensing that, tried to make his presence as unobtrusive as possible.

When Jeff excused himself from the table as soon as he finished eating, his mother foiled his escape by announcing brightly, "It's such a sticky night, let's all have iced coffee and cake out on the veranda, shall we? No, Jeff, dear..." She waved him off. Jeff, who was already on his feet, offered his arm to her. "The professor will take me. You escort our darling Amelia, will you?"

It was such a blatant—and unexpected—effort at matchmaking that Amelia was hard put to repress a grin. But Jeff's expression was completely unreadable.

There was a great deal of clatter as everyone rose to go outside, with Jeff and Amelia leading. It seemed to her that Jeff had made a point of avoiding her at supper—all afternoon, in fact—and Amelia couldn't keep a touch of dryness out of her tone as she murmured, "So. Together again."

"So it would appear. We shouldn't make a habit of it, however. It doesn't reflect very highly on you."

She was startled. "What do you mean?"

"I mean, my dear," he replied smoothly, "as anyone will be happy to tell you, no young lady who values her reputation at all would spend more time with me than she can possibly help."

She laughed. The statement, in light of all her other problems, was so absurd that she couldn't help it. "I half think you're serious!"

He hesitated. "Surprisingly enough, I half think I am, too. And on that note..." He led Amelia to a chair and, releasing her arm, bowed politely. "I think I'd best leave you here, to much better company than my own."

And before Amelia could do more than utter a syllable of protest, he went down the steps.

Martha Craig professed dismay when she saw her son was gone. "Oh, dear," she fretted, "he's usually not so ill-mannered. Elliot, what do you suppose can have gotten into your brother?"

Amelia noticed a stiffness in Elliot's voice as he replied, "Nothing that wasn't always there, Mother."

"Well, really." She sounded hurt. "And after I had Cook make his favorite pound cake."

"It looks delicious," Amelia interjected. She felt as though she should defend Jeff, and the only way she could think of to do so was to change the subject. "Do you use lemon peel?"

Martha beamed at her. "Why, how did you guess? It's so dear these days," she confided, "that it's terribly extravagant of me to use it in a summer cake.... Come here, my dear, and sit beside me."

Amelia took the place beside Martha Craig on the wicker divan, folding in her skirts so there would be room for both of them. A servant brought them coffee and sliced cake. Martha waited until Amelia had tasted her cake and made the appropriate—and genuine—murmurs of appreciation, before she settled back with a satisfied smile and said, "It's so nice to have you here, dear. And now that you've recovered from your bout with the heat I can say you had me worried for a while, and that's the truth. Jeffrey seems quite taken with you."

It took a moment for Amelia to understand where the conversation was leading. "He's been very— kind."

"I understand you went driving this morning. Now, my dear, I don't wish to criticize, but tongues will wag. You will be more careful, won't you?"

"Well, I—"

"It's *so* nice to see two young people enjoying themselves. And don't you be fooled. It wasn't so long ago that I was young myself. You are fond of Jeffrey, aren't you, dear?"

Now Amelia began to understand, and she was so taken aback that she could do little more than stammer, "Well, I— Of course, I am—"

Martha Craig took her hand and squeezed it warmly, a contented smile on her face. "He's my oldest, you know, and will always have a special place in my heart. But I want you to know I quite approve, and

I'm certain your mother will, too. I'll write her in the morning."

Amelia didn't know what to say, and in the end she thought it wiser to say nothing. In light of everything else that faced her, a matchmaking mother was far down on the list of her worries. In fact, she would have been amused if she hadn't remembered the odd look on Jeff's face as he left her a few moments before. And she couldn't help wondering what the real Mrs. Landston would have to say when she learned that her daughter—who was no doubt safe at home right now—was practically engaged to Jeffrey Craig.

The impromptu party on the veranda turned out to be ill-advised as, with the setting of the sun, the mosquitoes came out in full force. They all moved inside where the bugs followed them through the open windows, and the others, who were apparently more accustomed to living in harmony with the insect population, continued with their evening's activities. Abigail began explaining the art of cross-stitch to Amelia while Amelia surreptitiously swatted moths and gnats and mosquitoes. When had window screens been invented?

After a while a pleasant breeze blew up and the bugs dispersed. Though earlier in the day Amelia wouldn't have believed she could ever find herself actually relaxing with these people, she did. There was only so much stress the mind could take, and she couldn't worry about everything at once. In a way the gathering reminded her of evenings in her grandmother's parlor—the women sewing, the men quietly playing cards, someone picking out a piece on the piano—and it was pleasant. She didn't think she could ever adjust to the deprivations and inconveniences of this century, but there was a possibility—a small one—that there were some things about it she might come to enjoy.

And then Amelia remembered. She was sitting there, squinting doggedly over the tiny cross-stitches Abigail had drawn on a piece of white fabric, listening to Benjamin's poor piano-playing in the background, and it came to her so suddenly that she stabbed her finger with the needle and had to swallow back a gasp—not of pain, but of shock. The song. Last night she had heard—she had *thought* she heard—a twentieth-century song whistled beneath her window. Hadn't she? But if she had...

Shortly afterward, everyone began to say their good-nights, but Amelia pretended absorption in her needlework and asked permission to stay downstairs for a while. Her head was spinning and she couldn't go upstairs with Abigail and lie in the dark and pretend nothing was wrong. She had to think.

But when she was left alone in the shadowy parlor, pacing back and forth and twisting the piece of needlework in her hand until it was so crumpled the pattern blurred, Amelia's thoughts grew even more jumbled. How could anyone who lived in 1870 have heard a song that wasn't recorded until the twentieth century? She had just come to accept the fact that she *had* been transported back in time. Now was she supposed to believe that it was all a mistake, a misunderstanding, a practical joke? But if it wasn't, how could she have heard that song?

Maybe she hadn't heard it. She had been half asleep; she must have imagined it. She must have heard what she wanted to hear; that was the only possible explanation. But...

At last she tossed the wrinkled scrap of material down, pushed open the wide front door and stepped out into the night. She didn't want to think about it at all; she just wanted to walk away and leave the confusion behind.

The fresh air did help put things in perspective. The rain had passed them by, but the breeze had a cooling tang to it. She took deep, calming breaths as she made her way down the steps, trying to push the problem out of her mind. Hadn't she dealt with enough today? How many more mysteries could she reasonably be expected to solve?

There was enough light even in the overcast sky to guide her across the lawn, and instinctively she made her way toward the building Jeff had called a summerhouse. It was a small, quaint structure, she could see as she got closer; a miniature of the main house with columns at the front and shutters all the way around instead of windows. The door was open, and she stepped inside.

As her eyes adjusted to the darkness she could see that it was furnished with sofas, tables and chairs in an inviting, comfortable arrangement. The shutters were open to admit the breeze and it was much cooler here than in the main house—thus, she supposed, the term "summerhouse."

She had taken one cautious step across the floor when a voice spoke from out of the shadows. "Here I am, doing my best to save your reputation, and you're going out of your way to ruin it."

Amelia suppressed a gasp. "Jeff! Why are you always lurking in the shadows? And anyway," she added, walking over to the window where there was more light, "my reputation is probably the only thing I'm not worried about right now."

"Oh?" He had been reclining on one of the sofas at the back of the room—probably napping, Amelia realized guiltily—until she had interrupted. He swung his feet to the floor and sat up, but didn't come toward her. "What are you worried about?"

Her laugh was stifled and mirthless. "How much time have you got?"

"Lately it seems like the only thing I do have plenty of is time. I'd just as soon spend it listening to your worries as anything else I can think of. Did something happen after I left?"

With another prickle of guilt, Amelia realized that from the moment she met him, she had done nothing but tell Jeff her worries—and he was not a man without troubles of his own. When she thought about putting her concern about the half-remembered scrap of song into words, the whole thing sounded foolish, the desperate aberration of an overworked imagination. So she replied, "It's nothing. And everything." She sighed and turned to face him, leaning against the windowsill. "I guess I'm not dealing with all this as well as I thought."

"I don't know. I thought you did quite well at supper. You seem to have made a champion of my mother."

His voice sounded easy and friendly—that of a different man entirely from the one he had been at the house. The anonymity of the darkened summerhouse, the unrestrained way in which conversation flowed back and forth between them, relaxed her. Her tone was light as she replied, "Maybe too much. She practically made me a gift of her oldest son after you left."

After a slight hesitation he said smoothly, "My mother is a dear soul who cherishes the notion that the right woman can reform me. I wouldn't let her put ideas into my head if I were you."

Something about the warning nature of his last words rankled Amelia, and she responded snappishly, "I don't need anybody to put ideas in my head, thank you very much. And I'm not the least bit interested in your mother's ambitions for her son's future happiness."

His soft chuckle embarrassed her, making her wonder if she had made too much of a simple comment. "Good for you," he said. His steps were silent on the stone floor as he rose gracefully and came over to her. "And now that you've set my mind at ease about your intentions concerning me, just what *are* you doing wandering around the grounds at this time of night?"

"It's not that late," Amelia replied uncomfortably. His nearness brought a sensation of warmth and the faint odor of shaving soap and cigar smoke—two scents she knew she would forever after automatically associate with him. She turned toward the window on the pretext of catching a cooling breeze; mostly she wanted to avoid the amusement in his eyes, which in the darkness of the summerhouse was somehow seductive.

"Besides," she said, "I couldn't sleep. I've got too much to think about, too many plans to make."

"Such as?"

She paused, for those were the very things she had been trying not to think about all afternoon. "Such as, where I go from here, what do I do, how do I make a living? I can't live off your charity forever, you know."

"Actually," Jeff informed her easily, "you could. Witness Professor Kane. Granted, he has some sort of income from his little books and lectures, but mostly he just lives here—off Mother's charity, some might say, though never to her face."

Amelia shook her head, her hands tightening on the windowsill. "I could never do that. For one thing, I'd go out of my mind with nothing to do. For another— Well, as soon as your mother writes her friend in Charleston, she's going to find out I'm not who she thinks I am. And then it will all be over."

"The first thing you have to understand about my mother," Jeff said, "is that she never writes to anyone. She always intends to, but never quite gets around to it. Besides, I've already told her you're not who you claim to be."

"You did *what?*"

"I told everyone my suspicions yesterday afternoon while you were napping," he responded, unperturbed. "It was a topic of conversation for a time, but as you can see, it made no difference. As far as they're concerned you're just a helpless female in need of comfort and assistance, which they're most happy to provide. It doesn't matter who you are."

"I . . . see." It took Amelia a moment to digest this unsettling bit of news. "Well, that's—generous of them, I guess, but it doesn't really change anything. I still have to find a way to support myself, and I don't suppose the pay would be too high for a food critic in this century."

"I could better tell you that if I knew what a food critic was."

"I could work in a restaurant," she mused. "I'm a good cook. Are there any restaurants around here?"

His look of amused tolerance gave her the answer she already knew. Besides, she doubted whether restaurant work would pay a living wage for a woman alone, either.

She looked at Jeff. "Well? Do you have any suggestions?"

"Frankly," he admitted, "I've never been faced with the problem before. But it seems to me, with your knowledge of the future, you would have some kind of advantage over other women in your position."

Though the suggestion was delivered tongue in cheek, Amelia seized on it immediately. Of course. She could invent something, or invest in something, or . . . But almost immediately her spirits sank and the disappointment was worse than if she had never had the hope at all.

She shook her head. "I don't know anything about science, or mechanics, and I never was very good at history. I wouldn't know an opportunity if I saw it. The California Gold Rush has already happened, hasn't it?"

He nodded gravely, but she saw the twitch of repressed laughter at the corners of his mouth.

She sighed. "You see? Besides, Captain Kirk would say I shouldn't do anything that would change history."

"Who is he?"

"He's—" But the prospect of trying to explain television to him, much less science fiction, completely overwhelmed her. "Nobody," she finished wearily. "Nobody at all."

"Well, then," Jeff said after a moment, "it seems to me you have only one choice. You'll have to marry someone."

Amelia knew he was trying to cheer her up, and in gratitude she managed a laugh. "Thanks, but no thanks."

"Fortunately," he went on, "you have a houseful of candidates right here, which is more than most women these days have. For example, my brother Benjamin. I admit he's a tad young, but he's energetic and seems quite taken with you."

She gave him a dry look. "If I were interested in a husband—which I'm not—I'd at least want him to be out of the schoolroom."

"All right, then." Jeff leaned one hip against the windowsill and reached into his pocket for a cigar. "Let's consider Colonel Talbot. Loudmouthed and pushy—"

"And old."

"But he's a widower, and well-set from what I hear. Of course, the children might be a problem."

"Not to mention the grandchildren." Against her will, Amelia was drawn into the game.

"On second thought," Jeff added, "I believe he has his eye on Abigail, and my first loyalty is to my sister. So perhaps we'd better strike him off the list."

Amelia was astonished. "Abigail! But she's half his age!"

He shrugged. "The best marriages are often May-December. And mother approves. Everyone has to marry someone, you know."

Amelia had to take a moment to digest this. Colonel Talbot and Abigail... She never would have guessed.

"Now I should mention that Elliot has more or less been keeping steady company with a girl from Roanoke, but he hasn't asked her yet, and—"

Amelia shook her head. "Elliot's too stuffy. We already decided that."

"And you can't be too particular," he pointed out. "That only leaves Sam Calvert, and he's a troublemaker if I ever saw one. Besides, he doesn't have any money of his own and you'd have to live with his stepmother."

Amelia shuddered. "I don't think so."

"Smart choice. She holds the whole family by the purse strings. And from what I can tell, even Sam doesn't like her."

Amelia glanced up at him. "You left someone out."

He didn't pretend ignorance, and as he looked down at her, all traces of playfulness slowly left his face. "That," he said quietly, "would be a very unwise choice."

He sounded so serious that Amelia was embarrassed again, and she tried to lighten the mood. "Your mother would approve."

Jeff looked down at the cigar he held, making no move to light it. "My mother," he said, "is the only one who has ever approved of me at all. Sometimes I think she's not very wise, either."

The game had gone sour. The silence that followed was long and heavy with questions he would not answer and she did not know how to ask. Amelia made the most innocuous comment she could think of. "What a pleasant place. It's cooler out here, too, I think."

Her voice seemed to draw him from a reverie, and when he looked up a frown still lingered between his brow—but only for a moment. He tucked the cigar back into his pocket and replied, "My brothers and I used to sleep out here in the summer. It was an adventure, because we knew we weren't allowed to, and you know how boys will always do exactly what they're not supposed to. Of course, we found out when we were older that our parents had known about it all the time."

Even that simple memory seemed touched with pain, for the smile that had begun the story faded into wistfulness at the end, and then regret.

Attempting to brighten the mood, Amelia teased, "And you still make an adventure out of sneaking out here to sleep?"

He forced a smile. "Promise not to tell."

But there was something sad about a man who didn't even feel comfortable enough with his family to sleep under his own roof. Amelia said hesitantly, "You don't like being around your family, do you?"

He walked away from her, and for a moment she assumed he wouldn't answer. Then he said, "It's more like the other way around. Not that I can blame them."

"Why?" she asked, curious, taking a step toward him. "Is it because of what you told me the other night..." How long ago that seemed! And how strange to realize that at that time she hadn't had the faintest idea that what he was telling her was the truth. "About being—wanted by the law?"

"That, my dear, is just the latest in a long list of my sins."

He paused before a narrow sofa and gestured to her. "I'm forgetting my manners again. Would you like to sit down?"

She had a feeling that he didn't really want her to stay; she had intruded into his privacy, and the polite thing to do would be to leave him alone. But she didn't want to be alone, and she couldn't let the subject drop.

She came over to the sofa and sat down. "Will you tell me about it?" she asked.

He perched on the arm of the sofa near her, taking out the cigar again. This time he lit it by striking a match on the heel of his boot, and in the brief flare of the light she noticed the hard angle of his jaw and the tense column of his neck. But his voice sounded nonchalant as he tossed the match away and replied, "It's a complicated story."

"I'd like to hear it."

The pungent aroma of smoke drifted through the air, and after a moment he leaned back, his rigid posture loosening up. "I'm not sure I can explain to you," he said thoughtfully, "what it's like growing up on an island. You love it and you hate it. You spend your life wishing you could escape but something about it keeps drawing you back. And I guess every man who's ever gotten the island into his blood thinks he's a law unto himself.... My pa was like that, and so was I."

He paused for so long that Amelia thought he would say no more. His head was bent as he studied the glowing tip of his cigar, and in the semidarkness his expression was remote.

Then he continued. "I was at William and Mary when the war broke out. It was my first taste of freedom and I was delirious. Right after Fort Sumter, Pa sent for me. I guess as far as Pa was concerned we had seceded from the Union before there even was a Union—" there seemed to be a trace of irony in his tone "—because all any of us ever heard from him was that this wasn't our war. We didn't have a stake, we were our own master, and Pa was determined to stay out of it. But I saw it differently. Or maybe I just couldn't stand the thought of going back home. I wanted adventure. And when the other boys trooped out of class to enlist, so did I.

"I saw my pa once after that, all dressed up in my gray uniform and as proud as sin, and from the way he acted you'd think I'd joined the Yankee side. Maybe to him it was the same thing. I guess all he knew was that I'd betrayed him, and he was losing a son."

Again there was silence. Amelia didn't have to guess what he was thinking this time. She could see it in his face, as clearly as if the gentle movement of the shadows across his face were the march of soldiers' feet. She wanted to reach out to him and share the pain, yet knew she couldn't even come close to understanding what he had been through.

His voice was regretful when he spoke again. "War wasn't the adventure I thought it would be. When I came home, Pa was dead and Mother was old, and my brothers were grown-up. Nobody ever said it, but they never forgave me, either. Pa had worked and grieved himself to death, and Elliot had lost his boyhood taking over what I should have done. Nobody needed me here—I was just a reminder of the way things should have been. So I lit out for Texas, like so many other former Southern gentlemen who had no place else to go, and once there, I just kept on moving, looking for adventure, I guess. Or maybe just running away."

He drew on the cigar. "I had my share of adventure, all right. Saw some sights, too. I even had a try at making a life for myself out there once, raising cutting horses. I had a nice little spread, some strong stock, and I've always been good at business. Pa used to say I had a knack for making money work for me. That's why we weren't hurt by the war any worse than we were—because I talked him into putting some money away in overseas investments."

He paused, and tapped the ashes of his cigar. When he went on his voice was matter-of-fact. "Anyway, I must've lost my knack, because I got caught in the middle of a range war and lost it all, and after that there never did seem to be any point in settling down again. And then I had the misfortune to be riding with a bunch of bad men. They took it into their heads to rob a train that was carrying some important local folks and an army payroll. But I'm not a complete fool, and when they made their move on the train I cut out the first chance I got—and got shot in the back for my trouble. I was lucky. They hunted down and killed the other three. They put me up at a local doc's house, which was a lot easier to break out of than a jail."

"Then you really are—" Amelia sputtered "—a wanted man."

He nodded. "The minute I step off this island."

"I don't understand," she said uncertainly. "Why don't the authorities just come and get you? Don't they know you're here?"

His smile was mirthless. "Maybe. Maybe not. But fortunately for me, the Yankees haven't quite got the hang of enforcing those laws they were so anxious to shove down our throats, and there's still a lot to be said for states' rights. It would be different if I was wanted for a crime that happened around here—then I'd have the local boys to contend with. But it's a big county, and the sheriff isn't too interested in something that might or might not have happened a thousand miles from here. So I'm safe, as long as I stay put."

She didn't understand. "But if you're innocent—"

He shook his head. "Being innocent and proving it are two different things. And the federal marshals aren't very understanding these days to men with Confederate war records. We're all considered traitors, you know."

The time gap was suddenly a real and tangible thing to Amelia, and it left her dazed. The story he'd told was not a fascinating scrap from some long-ago diary—it was real and immediate and had happened to *him*.

"And when you came home," she said softly, "nobody wanted you."

His cigar had gone out, and he stared at it as though debating whether to relight it. "You can't blame them. They've gone on fine all these years without me. Elliot's in charge now and he's done a good job. Maybe he's afraid I'll try to take over. He's got a right to be suspicious of me. Benjamin barely remembers me, and God knows what he's heard. And Mother— Well, she tries to pretend everything is just the way it should be, but I know what having me here must do to her. The rumors make me sound worse than Jesse James and she doesn't know what to believe. The funny thing is..."

But he didn't finish the sentence. He frowned at the cigar and tossed it out the window.

"What?" Amelia prompted softly. She ached to touch him, comfort him. She saw the loneliness in his face and wanted to ease it. But her uncertainty held her back.

"Nothing," he replied after a moment, not looking at her. "It's just that— After I was shot, and on the way back here, I had a lot of time to think. And it just seems funny that after all these years of roaming and all the wasted time, that just when I'd made up my mind that home was where I wanted to be..."

"You found out you had no home to go back to," Amelia finished for him. She knew that feeling. How very well she knew it now.

He looked at her with surprise. "Yes," he said simply.

Amelia lifted her hand then, and stroked his face— a gentle caress that was merely an extension of the deepening bond between them. Her fingertips trembled over the smooth contour of the arch of his temple, at the roughness of his lower jaw. He met her gaze, tenderly and with no reticence, and his hand slid lightly around her neck.

"Amy," he said huskily. "You are sweet."

Amy. The intimate shortening of her name, when he said it, sounded indescribably beautiful.

He moved down until he was sitting beside her, his thigh pressed against hers, his hands cupping her face. Her muscles, her pulse, the rhythm of her breathing responded to his nearness with an instinctive welcome. She threaded her fingers through his hair and when his face moved close to hers her lips parted, drinking in the touch of his breath.

The swift hot passion of the first time wasn't there, nor was it the secure retreat into an imagined fantasy, a brief encounter. This was real. The intensity was even greater, the straining need that pulsed between them was like a tide that pulled and surged. Jeff's hand tightened on her face but with an almost-imperceptible pressure; she could feel the slight tremor of the muscles in his arms as he restrained his embrace. His lips barely brushed hers, yet the caress sent waves of longing through her. Their exchange was a symphony of achingly controlled touches of breaths, lips, fingertips.

Every nerve in Amelia's body was on fire for him, yet something held her back, as it did him. This was too real, too soon...too powerful. When his hand trailed down her face and to her shoulders and he lowered his gaze, she wanted to cry out in protest, to draw him closer—but she didn't.

His hands tightened on her shoulders and he said hoarsely, "Go back to the house, Amelia."

Her fingers curled around his collar, holding on just briefly, then she made herself let go. Her own voice sounded unsteady as she replied, "Worried about my reputation?"

He lifted eyes to her that were serious, yet alive with the passion that made her blood race. "I'm worried about both of us. Anyway you look at it, nothing good can come from—" his eyes focused on her lips "—this."

She searched his face, unwilling to leave him, even though she knew he was right. It was too much too soon, and she was far too vulnerable; but she didn't want to let him go. She whispered, "Are you sure?"

Something flickered in his expression, too quick for full interpretation, but she knew its essence. And it made her heart pound with a painful longing.

Then Jeff's hands tightened on her shoulders again and he stood, pulling her with him. "Make no mistake about it, Amelia Langston," he said. "I will ruin you if I can. And next time, I may not be so noble."

He pressed a brief, hard kiss against her mouth, and then released her abruptly. "Now go," he told her roughly.

Amelia left, because for that one night, she had no choice. And because deep inside she knew, as must he, that their parting was only temporary.

EIGHT

Amelia wondered if there was some equivalent to jet lag that afflicted time travelers, or whether her frustrating inability to sleep was merely due to shock and stress...and memories of Jeff that kept tumbling around in her head and dancing through her dreams, leaving her wakeful, anxious, and more confused than ever.

She was up that morning long before the annoying crow of the rooster. She could hear the faint sounds of the servants lighting the fires and beginning the routine of the day, but the rest of the house slept on. She dressed silently in the dark and, careful not to disturb Abigail, slipped out into the dawn.

She started down the drive at a brisk pace and kept it up as the drive gave way to the hard-packed soil of the wagon trail that encircled the island. The air was cool, and the humidity didn't seem so high—although Amelia doubted that would last after the sun came up. As long as she kept to the center of the road she didn't worry about what might be lurking in the heavy undergrowth on either side.

When the sun was high enough to shed a yellow glow over the leaves of the trees that lined the trail, Amelia reluctantly turned and retraced her steps, feeling winded by the time the curve of the driveway came into view.

Just then she was startled by the unfamiliar sound of hoofbeats on the road behind her. She whirled and scampered to the side just as a large mottled horse came into view.

It was Jeff, who drew up sharply beside her and dismounted. "What's wrong?" he demanded. "What are you running from?"

Amelia tugged her skirt loose from an ensnaring bramble, feeling somewhat foolish—and flushed and confused and utterly delighted to see him. "I wasn't running," she answered. "I was walking."

He looked at her damp, flushed face and disheveled hair with concern. "You were walking mighty fast."

He was wearing a hat today—a Stetson type pushed back on his head—and a faded butternut jacket over a dark shirt and flannel trousers. His riding boots were scuffed and he wore a gun in a holster strapped low around his pelvis. The sight of him caused a shiver of pleasure. The hat shadowed his face and one strong, slender hand held the horse's reins. She couldn't help remembering the texture of his skin beneath her fingertips and the way his callused fingers had caressed her face last night. The memory brought a surge of longing. She quickly resumed walking.

"I need the exercise," she replied. "People in this century don't get enough of it. Well, I suppose the men do," she amended, and couldn't prevent a glance at his arms and thighs, taut muscled from riding. "But the women don't."

Leading his horse, Jeff kept pace with her. The concerned look in his eyes remained. "You're going to hurt yourself if you keep that up."

Amelia slowed her pace, not because she wanted to placate him but because the main purpose of her walk was no longer aerobic. The chirping and fluttering of the birds in the trees, the soft green-and-gold morning, the smell of marshes and lush growth—and Jeff beside her. The moment was too precious to rush.

"In this outfit," she admitted with a wry gesture toward her skirts and shoes, "you're probably right. I don't suppose there's any such thing as a nineteenth-century equivalent to jogging shoes?"

He shrugged. "Shoes are shoes."

"I wish I had a pair of pants," she said with an envious glance at his own attire. "Then I could run every morning."

He laughed—so loudly that Amelia was sure he could be heard all the way back at the house. "Now, that I would like to see!" he exclaimed, his eyes snapping. "No, I take that back," he amended with a lift of his hand as the excitement on her face warned him of what she was about to suggest. "I'm afraid a sight like that would stretch even my family's tolerance to the limit, and I'd hate to have them lock you away. I'm just starting to enjoy having you around."

Though it was meant to be an offhand comment, the words pleased Amelia, and when she looked at Jeff she saw that he, too, acknowledged the deeper meaning of the sentiment. For a moment his eyes softened and he looked as though he would say something more, but apparently thought better of it and looked away. Amelia tried not to be too disappointed.

"Exercise is healthy," she explained to him, adroitly picking up the threads of the conversation. "In fact, in my century it's become almost an obsession—for men and women. Everybody runs or walks or goes to the gym to work out. *Slim, trim,* and *fit*—the by-words of the modern generation."

He looked amused and disbelieving. "Women, too?"

She nodded emphatically. "Especially women. You Can't Be Too Rich Or Too Thin—that's the slogan."

He still looked skeptical. "Well, I wouldn't overdo it if I were you. In the present time, men like their women soft and round—not hard and stringy."

Amelia didn't know whether to deride him for the chauvinistic remark and be insulted by the adjectives, or to wonder whether, when he held her in his arms last night, he'd found her soft—and as yielding as she had felt.

In the end, the safest thing to do seemed to be to laugh. "In my time, a comment like that would get your face slapped, at the very least. At the most, the woman in question might flip you over her shoulder and throw you on the ground."

He laughed again. "Now I know you're fabricating!"

Amelia thought she'd better change the subject. "What are you doing out at this time of day, anyway?"

"Just looking around. It makes Elliot nervous if I do the rounds in the daytime. He thinks I'm looking for something to criticize. But I couldn't find anything wrong, even if I wanted to. He's done a good job."

There was a note of regret . . . and envy in his voice, but Amelia didn't comment on it. She knew too well how it must feel to have lost everything, to come home and find yourself an outcast.

They started up the drive in a comfortable silence. She was surprised when, a few minutes later, he inquired casually, "Are there any wars in your time?"

"No," she answered. "At least none that we're actively part of." Briefly she told him about Vietnam, and the two world wars. "Right now we have a few enemies, but no declared wars," she summarized. "At least there weren't any when I left."

He seemed interested. "Then what do the men do with themselves?"

"For adventure, you mean?" She smiled. "Oh, they run businesses and buy and sell stocks, build space shuttles and race cars and fly airplanes—but then, so do the women." And at his uncomprehending look, she couldn't resist adding, "Men also stay at home and raise children and keep house while the women work, if they choose to."

He shook his head skeptically. "For a moment there, you almost had me convinced."

Amelia looked at him, but saw that he was only teasing her—just as he had probably assumed she was teasing him. The hurt she felt was irrational. Of course, he wouldn't believe her. What man of his time would? But she couldn't stop herself from hoping.

She struggled to keep petulance out of her voice as she responded, "It so happens I was telling the truth. Why did you even ask? You're never going to believe anything I say."

He smiled. "I had nothing better to do, so I decided to think about it."

"Oh, well, I'm glad I can at least give you something to think about." This time there was no disguising the sarcasm.

"I'm a little out of practice," he admitted, "so you'll have to bear with me. But in thinking about it, I've got to tell you I've already spotted a couple of flaws in your story."

"Is that right?" But she really wasn't interested in his reply. He had made it clear that nothing she could say would convince him, and she saw no point in discussing the subject when his skepticism only depressed her.

"Aside from the fact that no woman, present or future, will ever be able to flip me over her shoulder and throw me on the ground—" he slanted her an amused look "—it seems to me that if you really had traveled back in time, and things really were as different where you come from as you claim, you would have noticed the differences much sooner. You didn't seem to think anything was particularly amiss when you first arrived here, and it wasn't until yesterday afternoon that you—"

"I explained that," Amelia said impatiently. "I didn't know anything was wrong at first because I thought it was all part of the game. We were all dressed in costume and the guests were supposed to be playing members of the Craig family for the mystery weekend—"

Suddenly she stopped. She felt as though the breath had been literally snatched from her lungs, and with such a force that it left her chest aching. "The mystery," she whispered. "It really happened...."

How could she have forgotten? How could she have gotten so caught up in her own problems that she had overlooked the one, the only, the biggest problem, the root of it all, the reason she was here...? Had shock pushed it aside? Had she deliberately blocked it out? A murder was going to take place here and she was walking among the people who would be caught up in it.

Her hand went to her throat, which was so dry she could hardly form words. "It really happened," she repeated dully. "*Will* happen...."

Jeff took a step toward her. "Amelia?"

She focused on him. "What day is it?" she demanded hoarsely.

Alarm was mingled with the frustration that crossed his face as he said, "Amy, don't—"

"June," she whispered. "The middle of June—"

"Amy, for God's sake, stop this!" He grabbed her wrist, but she was too distraught to notice the anxiety that sharpened his tone.

"No!" She jerked her hand away, trying to put it together. She pressed her fingers to her temples as though the motion could stop the desperate racing of her thoughts. "Three weeks early. It was the third of July and now it's the middle of June— It happened on the fourth of July...."

"Amy—"

"Jeff, listen to me!" He attempted to take her hands again but she jerked away, turning to him urgently. "Sam Calvert is going to be shot—murdered—and his mother's necklace, that diamond-and-ruby thing she was wearing at dinner the other night, will be stolen on the Fourth of July, less than three weeks from now, and…'' Even as she spoke, her voice was fading away. The words almost seemed to come from someone else's mouth and she heard them from a distance. ''You will be the one who kills him….''

She saw the anxiety in his expression change to incredulity and then, horribly, to contempt. His eyes grew cold, the lines in his face hardened to stone. Without another word he jerked on the reins of his horse and moved away with long, angry strides. She ran after him and caught his arm. ''Jeff, please—''

He flung her arm away with a motion so quick and so powerful that she stumbled backward. His face was angry. ''No! I've had enough, do you understand me? I've listened to your foolishness, I've played the game with you—God help me, there were times when I even wanted to believe you—but this is enough! It's not amusing anymore, Amelia, and I won't have it!''

''Jeff, stop! Listen to me! Will you just listen to me?''

She stepped in front of him, so that he had to either stop or allow the horse he was leading to knock her down. For a moment she wasn't at all sure which decision he would make.

Then he halted and she recognized the look in his eyes—which was not so much anger, though there was a great deal of that—as hurt. And betrayal. ''I thought you knew me better. I thought we both—'' But he broke off and jerked his gaze away. ''Obviously I should be more careful who I tell my secrets to.''

He started to move around her, but she slid a hand on his chest—then dropped it immediately at the look of cold disdain in his eyes. "Jeff," she pleaded, "I didn't mean... Why are you angry? I'm only telling you what I know!"

"And of course you know that I'm the kind of man who'd murder a guest in my own home over a piece of gaudy jewelry. Why not? Once a killer, always a killer. That's the kind of logic that almost got me hanged in New Mexico."

He pulled so hard on the reins that the horse snorted in protest, and this time Amelia moved out of his way. But only for a moment. She couldn't let it go at that. She couldn't let him walk away, thinking... She didn't know what he thought. She didn't even know what *she* thought.

She caught up with him in a few running steps. Her fists were clenched and her voice breathless, but determination fortified her. "I don't know what happened," she said. "I can't tell you that. All I know is that a hundred and twenty years from now, when this house is a hotel and a group of people come here to play out a mystery for the grand opening, the tourist brochures will say that on July 4, 1870, Sam Calvert was killed, his stepmother's necklace was stolen and Jeffrey Craig was accused of the crime." She had to pause for a breath. "And if you'll come with me I'll prove it to you...."

She didn't wait to see whether he followed. She closed the remaining distance from the house in half-running steps, garnering startled looks from the servants. She took the path that wound around the corner of the house and out of the corner of her eye she saw Jeff toss the reins to a boy who came running up to receive them. After a few strides, he was beside her, his expression closed but not quite as angry as before.

She plunged through the barren rose garden, swept past the sundial without looking at it, and when her surroundings began to look familiar she stopped. "The west garden," she said, breathing hard. "This is where it happened."

She recognized the fountain with its modest statue of the infant Cupid, the delicate wrought-iron benches, the flagstone pavilion with its red-tile roof...and the wide chimney rising against the wall. Quickly she went over to it, searching for the telltale scar, but the rose-colored brick was intact and marked by nothing more than weather and the remnants of dead ivy that had been pulled away.

Feeling foolish, she stepped back. "Of course, it's not here," she said with slow recognition. "It hasn't happened yet."

Jeff stood a few feet away, silent and watchful.

She turned to him. "I'm telling you, a few days ago—in 1992—there was a mark on this chimney, a scar from the bullet that killed Sam Calvert."

His face remained impassive.

She took a deep breath, fighting to stay calm—or at least to sound calm. "I promise you, Jeff, it happened. There's not much I'm sure about at this point—yesterday I wasn't even sure I was entirely sane—but this much I know—I *remember*. It happened."

She saw a slight easing of the severity of his expression. Then he said, "Why don't you tell me the whole story, from the beginning."

Amelia felt a measure of relief. The rage had gone from his eyes. At least he was willing to listen. She organized her thoughts very carefully, then began, "Mystery weekends are kind of a popular thing to do—people get all dressed up and play assigned roles and try to solve the mystery—usually a murder—before the weekend's over. Most of the time it's a made-up mystery, but this weekend, the grand opening of the Aury Island Plantation Hotel, it was to be a reenactment of a real murder that occurred a hundred and twenty-two years ago.

"My friend Peggy was assigned to play Abigail, and I . . ." She shivered a little as she realized how accurate her assigned role had proved to be. "I was just called 'the mysterious stranger.' I never got to meet any of the others, and all I know is what it said in the introductory brochure they gave us."

She struggled to remember the details, cursing herself for not having paid more attention at the time. "It said that Sam Calvert was shot and killed in the west garden on July 4, 1870, and that the motive was apparently a diamond-and-ruby necklace belonging to his stepmother and—and that eyewitnesses cast the blame on—" she swallowed "—Jeffrey Craig."

"I see." His voice was dry, but the tightening of his lips was not amused. "I presume I was tried and convicted of the crime?"

Amelia shook her head. "No. You— You got away. Neither you nor the necklace was ever found. Nor . . ." and against her will, her eyes strayed to the heavy pistol strapped to his hip ". . . was the murder weapon."

His eyes noted the direction of her gaze and darkened with impatience. But his fingers twitched defensively toward the weapon even as he said shortly, "Oh, for God's sake, Amelia, every man on this island owns at least one gun. You'd be a fool to leave the house without one. The brush is full of snakes and alligators, not to mention the odd cougar or bear. Even you should know a man doesn't go riding in the country without a pistol."

She shook her head helplessly. "I don't know anything—except what I just told you."

He gave her a long, penetrating look. She wanted to hide from it, she felt herself withering away beneath it, and yet she met his gaze. "Just tell me this," he said calmly. "Do you really think I'm capable of robbing and killing a man in cold blood?"

Once, the answer to that had seemed simple. Of course, Jeffrey Craig was guilty; the truth had been so obvious it had taken all the fun out of the mystery. But that was before she knew him, before she had looked into his eyes and understood the essence of the man.

She knew the next words she spoke would be among the most crucial of her life. But she couldn't tell less than the truth. "I think...you're capable of killing, if you had to. If circumstances forced you to. But no," she continued, with complete honesty, "I don't think you're guilty of this."

Nothing registered in his expression except a flicker of acknowledgement in his eyes. "Well, then. It looks to me like there's no point to your story."

He started to turn away, but Amelia stepped quickly toward him. "The point is," she insisted, "that it *is* going to happen. And whether you're guilty or not, you're going to be accused of it, and be forced to run and—I don't want that to happen, Jeff!"

The desperation in her voice, the sincerity of her plea, caught his attention. His eyes narrowed as he looked at her, and gradually the last traces of anger and reserve left his face. After a moment he said gently, "Amelia, I don't know what could have put such an absurd story into your head. But if it eases your mind at all, remember I'm not quite the fool I act sometimes. I've got too much at stake to ever put myself in the position of being accused of anything, and even if I were, the last thing I would do is leave the island and walk right into the hands of the law.

"Don't you see," he insisted with a growing exasperation as she began to shake her head, "there are too many things that don't make sense. Why would anybody here want to steal the Calvert woman's necklace—much less kill for it? I know all these people. They're all gentlemen and none of them has any use for a fancy piece of work like that. Besides, they couldn't hope to get off the island with it. The whole notion is ridiculous."

But Amelia couldn't miss the apprehension that shadowed his features as he looked again at the chimney and followed its progress to the second story, where, Amelia noticed for the first time, a set of steps led from the second-floor gallery to the ground at the corner of the building. "What?" she insisted anxiously. "What are you thinking?"

His expression was guarded. "It's just that the Calverts are staying in this wing, and if anybody was going to try to steal the necklace, the logical thing for him to do would be to leave by the outside stairway to this garden. But I guess you knew that."

She shook her head slowly. "I didn't know that." And she looked at him in despair. "Oh, Jeff, please, don't you understand? A man is going to be killed, and you're going to leave here!" At that moment there was no question in her mind which of the two events was most significant to her, and she made no effort to conceal her feelings. "Jeff, you're the only one who— You can't leave! What will I do if you leave?"

He took a step toward her. Curving his forefinger under her chin, he lifted her face. All the despair and desperation she felt, plus less defined but equally intense emotions, were evident in her expression. He read them, and she let him. And she drew courage from the tenderness she saw in his eyes.

"I would never leave here," he told her quietly. "Not like that."

"You would," she insisted miserably, "if you had to—to save your life, or to protect someone, or— Oh, Jeff, what am I going to do without you?"

He seemed to move imperceptibly closer, as if to take her into his arms, or kiss her, and for just an instant, Amelia's breath was suspended.

And then he smiled and slipped his hand around her neck in a brief, affectionate caress. "I'll tell you what," he said lightly. "If I am forced to go on the outlaw trail again, I'll be sure to take you with me."

For a moment she felt euphoric. And even though desolation soon settled over her again, she managed a weak smile. "Sure. Just what you need. A twentieth-century crazy woman slowing you down while you're running for your life."

"If the crazy woman really can predict the future," he replied equitably, "she just might be worth having along. Now—'' he touched her shoulder lightly ''—I don't know about you, but my imagination has had more than enough exercise for this hour of the morning. Let's go in to breakfast.''

Her shoulders sagged in agreement, but her steps were reluctant, and he stopped to look at her. Once again she saw him struggle to find some way to offer her comfort in a situation he found utterly incredible. Once again she felt tenderness and admiration for his efforts.

He said patiently, ''Amy, look. Even if everything you say is true—even if you have some kind of second sight or...'' He wrestled with the words. ''If you *have* come from the future—what good does brooding about any of it do? Can you change anything?''

Deep in her heart, Amelia suspected that Captain Kirk was wrong; no one *could* change history. It had *happened,* and no amount of intervention could undo it. But if that was true, in less than three weeks Sam Calvert would be dead and Jeffrey Craig would be gone. What's more, no one had ever said what happened to the mysterious stranger....

''I don't know,'' she said. ''But what good is knowing if I can't do anything about it?''

''You don't really know anything,'' he pointed out. She could detect a hint of exasperation in his tone. ''A stolen necklace, a man shot... You don't know who or why or how or even exactly when. What do you think you can do?''

''That's right,'' she said slowly. ''I don't know any of those things. That was the whole point of the mystery. But if I did—if I could somehow narrow down the suspects—maybe I *could* do something! I've got three weeks."

Noting his skepticism, she insisted, "It's possible, Jeff. I know it sounds crazy to you but it *is* possible." She gripped his arm urgently. "Don't you see? I've at least got to try!"

She *had* to try. Because if she didn't, she would lose Jeff forever. That much was certain. And that, she could not bear.

After a moment he slowly shook his head, and his expression was a mixture of weariness, exasperation and regret. "Yes," he agreed. "Knowing you, I suppose you do."

NINE

When Amelia first realized she had traveled back in time, the actual date seemed insignificant to her. What was three extra weeks in comparison to a lost one hundred twenty-two years? But now those extra three weeks became an obsession—they were, literally, the difference between life and death.

She spent every moment of the next eight days insinuating herself into the confidence of members of the household, listening, watching, hoping for some clue that would lead her to the identity of the murderer of Sam Calvert. While it seemed everyone had reason to dislike Sam, no one had a motive to kill him. And no one—if the evidence she had gathered was accurate—had any reason at all to steal the necklace.

To complicate matters, Amelia discovered that the people she had met on her first evening were not the only guests. Hardly a day passed that the ferry didn't bring a new group of visitors or take some away. So she couldn't be at all sure who would even be present on the Fourth of July; maybe the person who was to kill Sam Calvert hadn't even arrived yet.

But Amelia wasn't discouraged; she couldn't afford to be. Somewhere there was a clue to the events of July fourth and she was the only one who could find it. Too much was at stake for her to fail now.

Elliot's girlfriend, Laura, was visiting from Roanoke along with her parents and her three young brothers and sisters. Martha Craig had suggested a picnic by the river, an outing that had been twice canceled because of afternoon rain, to commemorate their last day on the island—and, Amelia suspected, in hopes that the tranquil atmosphere of the shaded riverbank would bolster Elliot's courage toward voicing that all-important question.

So far the weather seemed to be cooperating, although a pile of fluffy white clouds low on the horizon held the potential for thunderheads late in the afternoon. Elliot walked with Laura on the riverbank. The other men set up the trestle tables that had been brought by wagon from the house, and the women unpacked the big hampers of food.

Martha Craig fretted, as she always did, about whether there would be enough, and Amelia laughed. "We've got enough here to set up camp for three days if we have to."

"I don't know. Children have such big appetites, and after all this work the men will be hungry— Salt. Did I remember to bring salt?"

She began to search frantically through a hamper, and Abigail calmly produced a covered salt bowl. "Here it is, Mother. You didn't forget anything. You even remembered things we don't need. Amelia and I will do this. Why don't you go see what Mrs. Calvert is complaining about?"

"Oh, dear." Martha cast a worried glance toward Mrs. Calvert, who was engaged in a tense conversation with Laura's mother. Both women's mouths were set and their bonnet strings were jerking. "Oh, dear," Martha murmured again. "I don't see why, just once, we can't sit down to a pleasant meal..." And she hurried off.

Amelia helped Abigail spread a long white cloth over the table and smooth out the wrinkles. Although Abigail was too much a woman of her times to ever be a close friend for Amelia, their relationship had improved enormously over the past week, and Amelia felt no constraint in asking her, as tactfully as possible. "Why did your mother invite the Calverts to spend the summer when they make everyone so uncomfortable?"

"They come every summer," Abigail replied. "I suppose because they have no place else to go. You might have noticed Mrs. Calvert is a little...abrasive." She offered an apologetic glance for even that mild condemnation. "They don't get many invitations. Besides..."

"What?" Amelia insisted, when Abigail seemed reluctant to finish.

"Excuse me, Miss Abigail, let me get that for you." Sam Calvert took the food hamper from Abigail and lifted it onto the table, smiling at her.

Abigail nervously returned the smile and Amelia understood why the girl had interrupted her sentence. But was her blush due to mere embarrassment over almost having been caught talking behind Sam Calvert's back? Or was it something more?

It would have been a farfetched suspicion if Amelia hadn't seen with her own eyes the way Sam's smile lingered when he looked at Abigail, and if Abigail hadn't gone on in a low, agitated voice when he left, "It's just downright silly, if you ask me. Who cares what happened in that old war, anyway? And just because Sam was in Europe...."

Amelia's curiosity leaped at the deepening of Abigail's blush when she said Sam's name. But she kept her expression innocent as she inquired, "Is that why everyone's so mean to him? Because he didn't fight in the war?"

Abigail gave Amelia a grateful look and moved closer. Perhaps it was Amelia's choice of the word *mean* that did it. "It was his stepmother's idea," she confided in an undertone. "She's a Yankee, you know, and can't be blamed for not having much sense. She took Sam over to England right before the war broke out and kept him there the whole time, even though he *wanted* to come back and fight for the south where he was born...."

Privately, Amelia observed that if a grown man had wanted to leave England, he surely could have found a boat to take him—even in wartime—but she kept silent.

"And it's not just that, either," Abigail continued sadly. She kept her eyes on the dishes of food she was unpacking, but her movements were slow. "People say that they made money off the war by selling out the Confederacy. That's ridiculous, of course, because Sam was over in Europe and the doctor was right here, taking care of Daddy all the time he was sick.... I guess that's why Mother feels obliged to be nice to his wife, because she feels she owed him for Daddy. But it's not very popular to be rich these days, and the way

Mrs. Calvert flashes around all that fancy jewelry, it's no wonder people talk.''

Amelia started to point out that the Craigs were rich—at least by the standards of their inland neighbors—but decided against it. She had enough to think about as it was, and there was still one more thing she wanted to pursue.

"Mr. Calvert—Sam, that is—certainly seems like a nice young man," she commented, unwrapping the cloth that covered a shank of ham.

Abigail's eyes blazed with defensive agreement. "He is, isn't he?" she insisted. "A man can't help who his parents are and I don't see why we can't—"

She broke off, and Amelia was so startled by that unexpected display of spirit that at first she couldn't think what to say. "Are you and he—" Delicately, she searched for the proper old-fashioned term. "That is, is he courting you?"

"Goodness, no!" Abigail's face went scarlet, and she fussed busily with a basket of rolls. "He would never— And my brothers would have his hide if he did— And I certainly...! It's just that he's been here every summer, and people do get to know one another...."

Suddenly she stopped, and looked at Amelia with more than a trace of defiance in her eyes. "The truth is," she said courageously, "if he ever did come to me, I wouldn't turn him away. And if you think I'm bad for saying so, then I don't care!"

"I don't think you're bad," Amelia gently assured her. "I think a woman has a right to care for whomever she pleases, no matter what other people say."

Abigail's eyes misted briefly in gratitude, and she smiled. "Yes," she said softly. "I knew you'd understand." She glanced briefly over her shoulder, and Amelia didn't have to wonder who she was looking at. Jeff was busy with the other men, carrying down chairs and cushions from the wagons, and it was to her brother that Abigail's gaze had shifted.

It was Amelia's turn to be uncomfortable, and she busied herself by searching in the hamper for napkins. She wondered what Jeff would say if he knew where Abigail's interests lay, and she didn't want to be accused of fostering a romance that really was none of her business—especially considering what she knew about the future. That realization caused a small shiver to go through her, and she said guiltily, "Of course, there's nothing serious between you and—"

A quick warning look from Abigail caused her to break off as Colonel Talbot approached. He bowed to the two of them, but his eyes were on Abigail. "Mighty fine spread, Miss Abigail," he said indulgently. "Mighty fine. I was wondering if you would do me the honor of taking the meal with me? I've got us a nice little spot under that chestnut there—"

Abigail's smile was forced. "You're very kind, sir, but I've promised my brothers I'd sit with them. And Amelia," she added quickly.

The glance the colonel directed at Amelia was of barely disguised hope. He paused a moment, as though waiting to be invited to join them, but Amelia said nothing. The silence was uncomfortable until he turned back to Abigail.

"Maybe a walk by the river afterward," he suggested.

Abigail was obviously trapped. "That would be lovely," she said weakly.

He bowed and departed, and Amelia tried to smile at Abigail. "You certainly do have your share of admirers."

Abigail's expression was fierce as she turned back to the basket. "I'll never marry him," she said lowly. "I don't care if I'm an old maid. Maybe other girls have to take what they can get these days, but I'm not going to be tied down to an old man who doesn't know how to talk about anything but the war, and I get so *tired* of hearing about it. Mama says I shouldn't keep putting him off, but I keep hoping—"

She broke off, and Amelia understood. Given a choice between Colonel Talbot and Sam Calvert, she supposed that she, too, would have waited for the younger man—no matter how undesirable he might be in other respects.

But Sam Calvert was destined to die. Knowing that, she couldn't in all conscience encourage Abigail's infatuation with him. She didn't want Abigail to be hurt, even though it was probably already too late. Amelia said hesitantly, "You know, sometimes a woman has to be practical. I'm sure the colonel is a nice man, and—"

"Money isn't everything," Abigail interrupted tightly. "A lot of people don't have money these days. And I'll tell you something else—I don't think the colonel is nearly as well-off as he pretends. I heard the bank wouldn't lend him any more money, and the rumor is that he might have to let that big old house of his go for taxes, so in that respect he's not much better off than Sam, is he?"

Something nudged at the back of Amelia's mind, but she couldn't quite grasp it. She was too concerned for Abigail at that moment to give it much thought, and she said anxiously, "But there isn't really anything between you and Sam, is there?"

Abigail kept her gaze fixed determinedly on her work. "There could be," she answered with a grim set to her mouth, "if Sam could ever get away from that woman's apron strings. He told me one time that if he could only get some money of his own, he'd buy a place out west, a little ranch, and start a family.... But until then, he's not free to do anything."

Martha Craig came bustling up then, and Amelia was glad they had to let the subject drop. Her throat was tight as her mind raced with possibilities. A young man wrestling against the weight of his mother's power and the shame of his own past... She remembered Sam Calvert's display at dinner the first night she arrived. "I'm as good a Confederate as any of you," he had asserted. He sounded like a young man with a great deal to prove, and that kind of desperation could easily lead him to a display of false heroism, especially if the love of a young lady was involved. Everyone hated Sam Calvert, and if they ever found out that he was secretly courting the daughter of one of their finest families... Well, stranger things had happened. That *had* to be it—something to do with Sam Calvert and Abigail....

Of course there were still a lot of things that were unexplained; how the necklace fit in, for instance, and who had done the actual shooting. But she had discovered a major clue, she was sure of it. Maybe it *was* possible to change the future. And maybe, just maybe, she had taken the first steps toward doing so.

Cushions and blankets were set up under the trees for the young people while the matrons settled in the comfortable chairs far enough from the river to gossip comfortably but close enough to keep an eye on the proceedings. Amelia ended up joining Abigail and Benjamin under a spreading oak tree on the riverbank, away from the others.

Amelia watched Jeff fill a plate for his mother and himself, feeling like a twelve-year-old in the schoolyard wondering whether the object of her latest crush would share his lunch. She was embarrassed when Abigail, noticing the direction of her gaze, lifted her hand and called Jeff over.

For a moment Jeff hesitated, and Amelia half hoped he would refuse the invitation. Then he bowed to his mother and brought his plate over to the oak tree. Once there, he made no pretense of wanting to join his sister and brother, but sat down beside Amelia on the blanket. Predictably, Amelia's pulse speeded with gratified excitement.

She was wearing a buttercup-yellow muslin gown sprigged with black. The wide black sash drew attention to a tiny waist, and the heart-shaped neckline was trimmed with cream-colored eyelet lace. Lace draped the hem and the yards of material that were loosely gathered over the back bustle, and gave a romantic flourish to the short, puffed sleeves. The brim of her big straw hat was tilted away from her face and its wide black ribbon was tied at a cocky angle to the side of her chin; she had even managed to coax her hair into three fat ringlets, which were pinned at the ear and bounced over her collarbone. The ritual of dressing for the picnic had taken over three hours—a process that would have previously appalled her but evidently was routine to ladies of this century. And when she saw the way Jeff looked at her, she decided it was definitely worth it. She felt beautiful.

Though his eyes were busy inspecting her face, the curve of her shoulders, and the heart-shaped portion of bare chest exposed by the neckline, his voice held a teasing tone as he commented, "My mother tells me you practically prepared the meal single-handedly."

One unexpected side-benefit of her "journey" was the opportunity for Amelia to study firsthand the original recipes that had developed into her favorite kind of cooking—Southern country/Chesapeake Bay cuisine. She spent an inordinate amount of time in the kitchen and had become a favorite of the cook, who often let her roll out bread dough or ice a cake but who would not, under any circumstances, tolerate any interference with Miss Martha's time-honored "receipts."

Amelia replied, "I told you food was my speciality. But the cook wouldn't let me do anything but watch."

"You made the tea cakes," Abigail pointed out, obviously trying to impress her older brother for Amelia's sake.

"And they're delicious," Benjamin put in with a grin. "I sneaked a few out of the basket."

Amelia wanted to point out that, with a pound of fresh butter and almost as much sugar to the dozen, they very well *should* be delicious, for the cook had watched her with the eye of a hawk, surreptitiously adding ingredients when Amelia tried to cut down until Amelia had given up in exasperation. But she accepted the compliment graciously, and answered only, "Your mother's receipts are wonderful."

"Mother says it's so unusual to find a girl who really likes to cook these days," Abigail said, again directing the comment toward Jeff.

Amelia was amused, both at the quaint attempt at matchmaking and at the comment itself, which would not have been out of place in the twentieth century. She answered, "My mother always said that all it takes to make a good cook is a woman who likes to eat. I used to be fat," she confessed.

Abigail's eyes widened with surprise, and Benjamin looked embarrassed; apparently, a woman's figure was not something that was discussed in mixed company.

But Abigail was too intrigued to be tactful, and she inquired sympathetically, "What happened? Did you fall ill?"

Amelia smiled. Secretly she was proud of the fact that, although Abigail was far from fat, she herself could fit easily into the other woman's gowns without the help of the corset Abigail struggled into every day. "No," she answered. "I stopped eating so much."

That was an effective conversation-stopper, and Abigail turned back to her plate with less enthusiasm than before. Amelia could feel Jeff's amusement, but he said nothing.

The rest of the meal passed easily, with Benjamin and Abigail carrying the burden of the conversation. But it was pleasant brother-sister talk, with occasional teasing and affectionate banter into which even Jeff was eventually drawn. The entire atmosphere—

the cool riverbank, the friendly knots of people, the informal chatting—was peaceful and benevolent; and for the first time, Amelia actually saw Jeff relax with his family. She understood then, as she never had before, the sadness that came into Jeff's eyes when he talked about the past. Meanwhile, over the last week, even she had been embraced by the affectionate warmth of his family.

As soon as they had finished eating, Abigail suggested to Benjamin, "Come on, let's go look at the dessert table."

"I'll get it," Benjamin volunteered gallantly, and got to his feet. "Ladies, what's your pleasure?"

"Jeff," Abigail said pointedly, "will fetch Amelia's dessert."

When Benjamin started to protest, Abigail nudged his ribs with her elbow and smiled benignly at Amelia. After a moment, Benjamin followed his sister, with obvious reluctance, back to the tables.

Amelia chuckled, and glanced at Jeff through narrowed eyes. "Do you ever get the feeling we're being thrown together?"

Jeff set his plate aside and leaned his shoulders back to rest against the trunk of the big tree. His smile was hard to read. "I don't think anyone has to go out of his way to throw us together, do you? We don't seem to be able to stay apart."

That was an odd thing for him to say, and Amelia didn't know quite how to respond. "I thought you'd made a vow to keep your distance from me."

"I want it to be remembered," he assured her through a mild twinkling of his eyes, "that my intentions were always noble. But that won't be the first vow I've ever broken. Did you really make the tea cakes?''

She laughed, startled and relieved at the change of subject. "I did. And I've discovered something else— what it is I can do to make a living in this century.''

"Cook?" he suggested lazily.

She answered, "No— Well, yes, in a way. I was thinking what I'd really like to do is run a hotel like this—an inn, I guess you'd call it. To offer the same kind of hospitality and good meals your mother does, making sure people feel welcome. I would enjoy that, Jeff. I really would.''

"Can this be the same woman who only a few days ago swore she didn't know what she would do without me?" he murmured teasingly. "Less than a week, and already you've turned into one of those dreadfully independent businesswomen.''

She glanced away uncomfortably—not because she was embarrassed, but because the words were more true than ever. "I have to make a living," she said.

"Why a hotel? Why not a home?''

"Because—''

"I know, I know. Because you have to make a living. That independent streak of yours can be a curse, you know. Just where do you intend to get the money for this fine hotel?''

She sighed, deflated. "I don't know. Nowhere. It was just an idea. Just a way of—I don't know—trying to convince myself there's something I can do in this time, some way I can be happy.''

His voice was serious. "Aren't you happy here, Amy?''

She looked at him, and the melancholy that had hovered over her a moment ago fluttered away like clouds dispersed by the wind. In her own time, would she ever have had a chance of meeting a man like Jeff? In her own time, a man like Jeff couldn't even exist. Was she really so unfortunate, after all?

"Today I'm happy," she replied. "This minute I am. But tomorrow..." She hesitated, trying to put it into words. "There's so much I miss. Little things, like toothpaste and television. And big things, like—" she smiled "—family, friends.... Some people dream of going back to a simpler time, but I've never been one of them. I'll never really like it here. I'm a freak, a misfit in this time."

Jeff shook his head in gentle amusement. "A freak? Hardly that. There are some things about you that are—surprising. But you're not as much a misfit as you think. As a matter of fact, you'd fit right in with the women out west."

That was something Amelia had never thought about before. The West had always been more progressive than the East—most particularly the Southeast—and that would go a long way toward explaining why Jeff didn't find her manners and her opinions as startling as he might have otherwise. She said, only half joking, "Maybe I should go west, then."

"I hope you don't. I should be obliged to follow you, and I don't think that would be too good for my health."

She caught her breath, looking at him quickly. It was impossible to tell how much teasing lay behind the comment. She said, "Would you, Jeff? Would you follow me?"

"Of course, I would," he answered with easy sincerity. "I couldn't let you make the trip alone, and who else can you trust with your secret?"

A warmth spread through her that was as sure and gentle as an embrace. Maybe she would never be completely happy here, maybe she would never belong. But she was not alone. And that knowledge held such promise that the rest was almost worth it.

Suddenly flustered, she started to rise. "I suppose someone should start clearing all this stuff away."

He lightly placed his hand over hers. "The ladies don't bother with that. The servants will be down to take care of it after a while."

"Oh, yes. I keep forgetting." She settled back down and his hand remained over hers, holding it against the soft cushion of grass with no pressure at all, just a wonderful warmth that traveled up the length of her arm and tingled in her throat. "I'm not used to the life of the idle rich."

He chuckled. "Is that what we are?" His hand left hers to pluck a dandelion from the grass near her skirt, twirling it absently between his fingers. The color was almost the shade of her gown, and he held the flower briefly against the material of her skirt as though to ascertain the fact for himself. "It's not always such a bad thing, I reckon—being idle. It just takes some getting used to."

He turned the flower in his fingers, brushing its petals along the back of her hand as it rested on the grass. The feathery caress made her skin prickle, and the indolence of it—so unlike Jeff—made her smile. "It's good to see you relax for a change," she said.

He tossed the blossom away. "That's something else that takes some getting used to. Especially," he added, with a lazily hooded glance toward her, "since you showed up."

But Amelia didn't want to be reminded of unpleasant reality on such a fantasy-perfect day as this. Her gaze drifted over the scene—children tossing a cloth ball back and forth on the rich green riverbank, matrons chatting lazily in the sun, Elliot sitting at the feet of Laura in her pink dress and smiling at her in much the same way that Jeff was smiling at her now.

She asked, "Are Elliot and Laura really going to get married, do you think?"

"Of course. It's just a matter of time."

Amelia couldn't prevent a trace of wistfulness from shadowing her smile. "Things sure were a lot simpler—now." She had to correct her tense at the last minute. "A man and a woman are attracted to each other and as long as their families approve there's no problem. They get married and stay married, and that's that."

"And it's different where you come from?"

She laughed softly. "Infinitely."

"How?"

The curiosity in his tone might have been genuine or it might have been indulgence, she couldn't tell. "Oh, relationships are much more complicated in the twentieth century. Everyone has to talk about his or her feelings, and personal space, and psychological needs, and ability to commit. And by the time all the talking is done, most of the emotion is gone."

Jeff said, "Tell me about this fellow of yours." There was no mistaking the interest in his tone this time. "Why did you leave him?"

"Bob?" Amelia was surprised. She had almost forgotten having mentioned him to Jeff. And even more surprising was the revelation that Bob was the one thing from the twentieth century she did not miss—and she hadn't even thought of him in so long it was hard to even remember his face. She said, "I didn't leave him—he left me. He thought I was boring."

A furrow of astonishment and disapproval appeared between his dark brows. "Boring? Now, that I can't believe. What kind of idiot was he?"

Though flattered by his defense of her, Amelia had to laugh as she shook her head. "But I was—am. In comparison to other twentieth-century women I'm not very exciting at all. You only think I'm interesting because I'm different. Besides . . ." She glanced down at the pool of bright yellow her skirt made on the grass, absently picking off a leaf that had drifted onto the fabric and marred the effect. "I have a tendency to— cling to things, and people, just because they're familiar. It wasn't a good relationship for either of us, but I just couldn't let it go." She lifted her shoulders in what she hoped was a light, dismissive gesture. "No man likes a woman who clings to him."

The frown between Jeff's eyes had deepened. "The men must be pretty strange where you come from."

She smiled wryly, remembering when she had said much the same words to him. "Some of them are," she admitted. "Most of them are just doing the best they can in a very confusing world."

Jeff plucked a blade of grass and examined it for a long time. Then he tossed the blade away abruptly and said, "Well. We all have our crosses to bear."

He stood, extending his hand to hers. "It's going to rain. Let's take a walk before it sets in."

It wasn't so much a suggestion as a demand, and Amelia couldn't have refused if she had wanted to. She allowed Jeff to assist her to her feet. Only a slight speeding of her pulse betrayed the pleasure she felt at the prospect of being alone with him.

They walked along the edge of the riverbank where for the most part they were in full view of the others. Jeff didn't offer his arm—possibly in deference to the curious eyes that were watching—and he didn't speak for a long time. A kind of brooding silence seemed to have come over him that matched the changed mood of the day. There was a muted sound of thunder, and the river had grown dark and choppy. Occasional flashes of bright sunlight broke through the clouds, adding an eeriness to the wind-tossed leaves and rippling grass.

She couldn't help noticing that she and Jeff weren't the only ones who had taken advantage of the relative privacy offered by a walk along the bank. Aside from Elliot and Laura, Abigail had apparently been pressed into keeping her promise to Colonel Talbot. They walked slowly through the trees lining the riverbank; the colonel had tucked Abigail's arm possessively through his and even at this distance, Amelia could see that Abigail was stiff with unhappiness. The sight of them blotted the pleasure Amelia could have taken from this time alone with Jeff, bringing to the forefront many more unpleasant realities.

At last she couldn't keep her suspicions to herself any longer and asked, "Jeff, how would you feel if you knew Abigail was interested in Sam Calvert?"

He shot her a sharp look. "She told you that?"

Amelia hesitated, knowing she had made a mistake. "In a way. It's nothing serious, just—"

"And what about him?" Jeff's eyes were dark and his mouth set angrily. "Has he dared—"

Amelia hadn't expected a reaction quite that strong, and she shook her head quickly. "No, nothing like that. I'm sorry I brought it up, Jeff. It was silly. Forget it."

Jeff's eyes searched the area behind them until he found Abigail and the colonel. It was an unfortunate coincidence that Abigail happened to be looking toward the picnic area just then, where Sam Calvert was standing alone against a tree, gazing back at her. Jeff's eyes narrowed, and he took a step away from Amelia.

"Maybe I'd better have a word with my sister," he said.

"Jeff, don't." Anxiously, Amelia laid a hand on his arm. "If you do that she'll know I told you, and I shouldn't have. I only brought it up because..." She let the sentence trail off.

Jeff studied her intently, and the impatient frown in his eyes made her want to shrink. "Because what?" he demanded. And slowly the scrutiny in his eyes cleared into understanding that was almost worse than his anger had been.

"Because," he said flatly, "you wanted to see if I'd be mad enough at Sam Calvert to shoot the poor man for making advances toward my sister."

Amelia dropped her gaze miserably.

"For God's sake, Amelia, this is 1870." There was disgust in Jeff's voice. "Duels have been outlawed. And no matter what you hear about hotheaded rebels, gentlemen don't solve their problems with a gun. When are you going to let go of this ridiculous theory of yours?"

"It's not ridiculous!" she cried, insistence and impatience sharpening her voice. "It happened!" But Jeff's expression was contemptuous, and she started walking again.

All the glory had gone out of the lovely day, blotted out as abruptly and as thoroughly as the scuttling clouds had obscured the sun. She had known it couldn't last—not with her certain knowledge of the future hanging over them like a specter. But perhaps for a few more minutes she could have pretended. . . . Instead, she had deliberately shattered the harmony that had grown between them. She hated herself for that; but for her own sake, and Jeff's, what else could she have done?

Jeff walked beside her, his hands clasped behind his back and his shoulders stiff. When the wind tousled his hair he didn't lift a hand to smooth it, but kept his head lowered and his eyes on the ground.

After a long time he said, in a rather subdued tone, "You don't have to worry. I'm not going to shoot Sam Calvert. I'm not even going to talk to him. It's none of my business anymore, what my sister does."

A rush of shame went through Amelia for having made Jeff think that she doubted him, and her own voice was as quiet and as unhappy as his as she said, "I never thought you would deliberately hurt any-

body or—shoot in cold blood. It's just that sometimes circumstances—''

"No circumstances," Jeff said with a low, deliberate vehemence, "will ever persuade me to take up a
gun against another man again. Do you understand
that, Amelia?''

He turned eyes on her that were dark with a pain
deeper than any her accusations could have caused,
and cold with grim intensity. Guilt and anguish closed
her throat. Why was it that, in trying to help him, she
always ended up hurting him? Jeff was innocent. She
knew that in her very soul. And yet there was something—something she was overlooking, some clue she
couldn't quite grasp. She was close, she knew she was.
And she couldn't give up now. Her wits and her
knowledge of the future were Jeff's only hope. And
even if he ended up hating her for trying, she had to
find the answer that would save his life.

They walked against the wind. Gusts snatched at the
hem of Jeff's coat and whipped Amelia's skirt around
her ankles, only to die down for a moment or two before whistling through the trees again and sending a
litter of green leaves dancing across their path. Amelia could hear the distant sound of voices and movement as the wagons were hurriedly being loaded for
the return trip. She knew they should go back, but she
didn't suggest it. Neither did Jeff.

After a time she said quietly, "I'm sorry Jeff. I've
brought you nothing but trouble and unhappiness
since I came here. I've dragged you into my problems
and told you wild stories about the people you care
about, and made you worry about things that you
shouldn't even know and . . . I'm sorry.''

Jeff hesitated, and then he answered softly, "Oh, you've brought me a great deal more than trouble." His head was still lowered, his eyes thoughtfully on the ground, but there seemed to be the faintest trace of a rueful smile at the corners of his mouth. "You've brought me imagination and possibilities and, yes, even adventure. You've made me think about things that can't be and wonder if they could. You've made me remember, for a little while, what it was like to be a boy when nothing was improbable and everything was big and exciting and mysterious and there were no limits to what tomorrow might bring." He stopped and turned to her, his expression sober. "If nothing else," he said, taking both of her hands in his, "I will always be grateful to you for that, Amy."

The warmth of his hands on hers made her chest tighten, and the gentle sincerity in his voice produced a longing inside her. He could never know how deep a part of her he filled, how lost and empty she would be without him. She wanted to tell him. She wanted to slip her arms around his waist and lay her head against his chest and tell him...so many things. But she couldn't.

He must have read the yearning in her eyes, though she tried hard to hide it, for his face softened. The wind tugged a lock of hair from the pins and swept it across her throat; Jeff lifted his hand and smoothed it back. He said huskily, "Oh, you've brought me unhappiness. But not in the way you think."

His gaze searched her face, resting on each feature as though to memorize it, or caress it. Her breathing was tight with anticipation, or wanting, or dread—she couldn't be sure which. Her fingers tightened on his.

His voice was low, and when he spoke, everything else seemed to fade away—the slapping of the river against its banks, the swaying of the trees, the sound of distant thunder. There was nothing but Jeff; and his words tore at her heart.

"I've been running all my life," he said. "First from the island, then from the war, and finally from the mess I'd made of my own life.... I came back here because it was safe and I was tired and there was no place left to go. And then you came and made my safe corner of the world suddenly seem bigger than the whole universe, and I wanted...so much."

His hands slipped over her wrists and up her arms, resting on her shoulders as though to draw her close— or push her away. "You're looking at a man who's wasted his life, Amy, who's turned his back on everything that ever held any promise and just kept pushing on, looking for God knows what. I never regretted it, never wanted it to be any different—until now. I've used up all my chances. There's no place left to run. And what I want is to turn back the clock and erase the past, to do it all over again, to have just one more chance...for you."

Don't fall in love with this man, a voice inside Amelia's head whispered desperately. *You can't fall in love with him.* But against her will and without her permission, her lips parted and the word escaped, "Jeff..." Within that single, choked syllable was all the longing, all the pent-up need and all the hopelessness she fought so hard to keep repressed.

He looked at her, but not with joy—with despair. His fingers dug into her shoulders. "I have nothing to offer you," he said hoarsely. "I want to take care of you, to give you the things you need and that the men you've known before have been too stupid or too selfish to offer. I thought my life was spent until you brought your own brand of magic to it. I want to make you see how beautiful you are, how special. I want to protect you and treasure you and make a place for you here, with me.... But I can't."

Those three words were spoken quietly, but forcefully. Within them lay all the anguish and grief that was tearing at Amelia's heart at that moment. His fingers tightened on her shoulders and he repeated deliberately, as though each word were another nail in the coffin of a hope that must never be raised again, "Do you understand that? I *can't.*"

For a long time Amelia was held by the look in his eyes, by the firm, almost angry resolution there. And the torment that etched his face into stony lines was not his alone. If ever she had needed to be in his arms, it was then. If ever she had needed to comfort and be comforted, to pretend even for a moment that their combined strength could somehow form a defense against all that assailed them, it was then. *Hold me.* The words echoed inside her head, silently, desperately, and so loudly that surely he could hear. *Just hold me....*

But the only words she allowed herself to speak were a broken, "I know, Jeff."

The wind clawed at her skirt and blew a streak of moisture across her face—a tear, she realized numbly. Slowly the pressure of Jeff's fingers on her shoulders lessened, until she was standing alone. She lifted her hand to brush her cheek, then started walking back toward the others.

TEN

As soon as Amelia came within sight of what had been, only a few moments previously, the scene of a peaceful picnic, she knew something was wrong. The wagons were loaded and ready to go, but Elliot was quickly unfastening one of the horses from its traces. The women were huddled in a knot near the riverbank and the sound of sobbing was clear. Amelia quickened her step. Jeff, touching her arm briefly, ran ahead. After a moment Amelia picked up her skirts and followed him.

She arrived just as Laura's mother, covering her face with her hands, collapsed against Martha Craig's shoulder. "It's all my fault! I should have been watching them more closely. I—"

"It's little Pearle," Abigail quickly explained to Amelia. "She's wandered off and—"

"The meadow!" Laura cried. "She was talking about the wildflowers in the meadow—" She caught her skirts in her hand and turned to run.

"I'll go with you!" Abigail cried.

Jeff strode to the wagon and returned in a moment with a gun holster strapped to his hip. Elliot, riding bareback on a wagon horse, had a rifle gripped in his hand. "I'll go upstream," he announced.

Jeff's expression was grim. "I'll go down. Two shots if you find her."

Elliot took off at a canter and Jeff called against the rising wind, "You gentlemen get the ladies on back to the house before the storm breaks. We'll meet you there. She can't have gone far."

The child's mother broke into a renewed paroxysm of sobs, while the father insisted loudly, "A horse! I need a horse!"

Amelia said, "I'll take the path through the woods back toward the house. Maybe she went that way."

Jeff caught her arm. "Don't be a fool. We've got enough women wandering around here as it is. Go on back to the house with the others."

Amelia jerked her arm away. "Abigail and Laura won't make it a hundred yards in those corsets and slippers of theirs. I'm twice as strong as either one of them and you know it. Besides, if she's hurt or—" She swallowed. "The only way anyone will ever find her in the woods is on foot, and you need more than one person searching."

She didn't give Jeff time to think of an answer to that. She pushed quickly past him and into the woods.

Jeff was probably right; they had enough people searching and as soon as the rest of the men got to the house they would return with horses and comb the area far more thoroughly than she could on foot. But it went against her nature to stand idly by while others did the work; she needed to keep moving. At that moment the only way she could outrun the pain that was gnawing at her heart was to move and to move fast, to focus on something other than the desperation that threatened her when she looked into Jeff's eyes.

She tore her skirt away from thorny vines that snatched at it, pausing every few steps to call for the missing child. She hadn't gone more than a dozen yards before the stormy gloom made futile any hope of spotting Pearle, but still she plunged on, calling even more loudly in hopes that the child would be able to hear her and respond.

The wind made a rattling, hissing sound through the trees, branches cracked and tumbled toward the earth. A sudden violent gust of wind snatched her hat from her head and sent it hurtling into the undergrowth. She didn't bother to retrieve it. A clap of thunder, very close, made her cower, but how much more frightening must this all be to a lost little girl? She stumbled on, pushing at low branches and clawing her hair away from her face, shouting for Pearle.

Then, from overhead, there was a noise like the roar of the ocean. Frightened, Amelia stopped and looked up toward the tops of the trees. It was so dark now she couldn't even see the movements of the trees as they were bent by the wind, but a crackling, splattering sound interspersed with the roar finally identified the noise—rain. She cupped her hands and shouted with all her might, but even she could hardly hear her own voice.

The roar of the rain and wind was suddenly muted, as though the storm was pausing for breath. She opened her mouth to shout again but then she heard a sound—two sounds, in close succession. Too sharp to be thunder, too definite to be a falling branch. They were rifle shots. The men had found the lost child.

Her relief over the fate of Pearle was short-lived. Amelia turned to go back the way she had come when the air was split by an ear-shattering crack. She watched in horror as the top of a bare, long-dead tree swayed, then crashed through the branches overhead, bringing down saplings and young pines in its wake as it landed, with a thud that shook the ground, not twenty feet in front of her. Choking on a cry of fright, she plunged back down the path in the direction of what she hoped was the house.

Before long, Amelia lost the path. And soon after, it seemed, the rain broke through the canopy of the trees in a drenching, driving torrent. The wind tore at her clothes and pushed her back one step for every two she took; it whipped her hair into her eyes and flung stinging pine needles and clinging, soggy leaves into her face. The roar of the storm grew deafening; she couldn't hear the crack of the branches until they fell right in front of her or, in some cases, right on top of her. The thunder gathered itself in low, echoing rolls and then exploded. And the lightning... It forked from the sky and flashed from the ground in blinding streaks and waves—a series of quick, brilliant illuminations that left the air hot and tasting of electricity and then subsided, only to revive when she least expected it.

She was running, stumbling and falling, then picking herself up again, sobbing and choking on the rain that filled her mouth. She could no longer see or hear, but she ran on, trying to escape the storm.

She began to cry out for Jeff. Jeff, who was strong enough to keep her safe, sure enough to take away her fears—Jeff who could never be hers because history had decreed that he couldn't stay. Jeff, whom she needed more than she had ever needed anyone or anything in all her life...

Gasping ragged sobs of breath, she wiped the water from her eyes and frantically tried to get her bearings. But again her vision was blurred by slashing rain, and all she could see were shadows of green and brown, bending and twisting with the wind. She plunged ahead but her foot caught on a fallen treetrunk. Stumbling, she cried out and flung her arms forward. Her hands met something solid: Jeff.

He shouted something at her but she couldn't hear over the roar of the storm. Water streamed from his hat and drenched his face, which was drawn with anxiety. It was the most beautiful face she had ever seen. She wound her fingers into the sodden material of his lapel and pressed her face against his chest, and she could have stood there forever, safe in the shelter of his arms. But he turned her away, bending close to shout something that she didn't hear. Holding her close with one arm around her waist, he urged her forward.

Amelia didn't know how long the last part of the journey took. Her lungs ached and her legs strained against the weight of her sodden skirts, needles of rain that felt like sharp stones battered her shoulders and tore at her scalp. It didn't matter. Jeff was there. And together they would find their way through the storm.

She hardly knew when they broke out of the woods and into a clearing, except that her feet moved faster and slipped less often, and Jeff's arm tightened around her in urgency. The rain was so thick she literally could not see her next step, and she didn't object when Jeff picked her up and carried her the last few strides.

He set her down on a hard stone floor, then turned to draw closed a set of doors. Still gasping for breath, Amelia drew her hands across her eyes and looked around. It took her a moment, in the gloom, to recognize the summerhouse.

The first thing Jeff did was to fling off his soggy and misshapen hat. Then he stripped away his sodden coat and tossed it aside. It hit the floor with a wet slap. Then he turned on Amelia, his eyes blazing.

"Are you crazy?" His voice was hoarse—with shouting, she realized distantly; shouting over the storm as he had searched for her. "Don't you know what could have happened to you out there? Why didn't you listen to me? Why didn't you stay with the women, where you belonged?"

His anger meant nothing to her. She stood there and looked at him, filling her senses with his presence. His shirt was drenched, the thin material molded to his chest and outlined the firm muscles of his arms. His dark hair was plastered to his scalp and forehead, and water dripped down over his cheeks. His face was pinched with worry. All she could say was, "I knew you'd come."

She took a faltering step toward him, and was swept into his arms. Crushed against his powerful chest, she heard the thunder of his heart pounding against her ear. His strong broad hands moved urgently over her back, cupping her neck, threading through her hair and caressing her scalp.

"You little fool," he muttered. His breath was still uneven from stress and exertion, and she could feel his muscles strain as he fought the urge to press her even closer. "You will drive me mad. Don't you know how worried I was—we all were?"

With a tightening of his muscles, he started to move away, but Amelia wound her arms around him with all the strength she possessed and gasped, "No! Don't leave me. Jeff, I'm so scared!"

He bent his head to hers; she felt the brush of his kiss. "It's all right," he said softly. "It's over now. I'm sorry I yelled at you."

Still she clung to him, trembling, her eyes squeezed tightly shut.

"There's nothing to be scared of," he insisted soothingly. "We're safe enough here. Everyone else is in the the house and that old place has seen worse storms than this. Nothing's going to hurt you now."

"It's not—the storm!" she managed through clenched teeth, trying to force back the shudders. But she couldn't let go of him, and she couldn't open her eyes.

"What, then?" Tenderly he cupped her face and tilted her head back, forcing her to look at him. "Why are you so afraid?"

"Because," she whispered, "you are going to leave me and there's nothing I can do to stop it and— Oh, Jeff, it's so hard not to love you!"

The next moment, everything was blotted out by the power of his kiss. The storm faded away. Uncertainty vanished and fear was swallowed up by the sweetness of his embrace. Jeff. That was all that mattered. He was here and she loved him and there was nothing to be afraid of.

He pushed back the wet, clinging strands of her hair with his fingers as his lips brushed her temples, her forehead, her closed eyelids. He whispered, "Ah, Amy. I don't have any self-control where you're concerned...."

Amelia placed her forefinger across his lips, stilling his words. His eyes closed as she spread her fingers over his face, tracing its planes and gentle hollows. She needed nothing at all as long as Jeff was here.

She said, "Jeff...I want to make love with you."

He opened his eyes. She saw yearning there, and torment, and reluctant denial. Yet his hands instinctively reached for her as she stepped away.

She unfastened the tapes of her skirt, then her petticoat and bustle, and let the garments fall in a sodden mass around her feet. Her fingers were surprisingly steady as she worked the small buttons of the bodice through the wet material, then slipped it off her shoulders. She stood in Abigail's borrowed underclothes, the wet lawn fabric clinging to her like a second skin.

Never had she been so bold before, so unashamed. But never had she been so certain before, either. And never had she looked into a man's eyes and seen the light that was in Jeff's. It went beyond passion, beyond desire. It touched her very soul.

He said huskily, "How can I help loving you?"

He took her in his arms and together they sank into the feathery softness of the sofa, lost in wonder and need.

When the last of their wet garments were discarded, their bodies warmed each other's, his hardness blending into her softness. As passion built, their movements grew more urgent; muscles strained and fingers tightened, and in Jeff's lovemaking Amelia sensed the same edge of desperation that was in hers. Arms couldn't hold tightly enough, mouths couldn't drink deeply enough, bodies couldn't meld closely enough. And their mutual climax sealed them for an eternal moment into one body and one soul. Yet they clung together, seeking more, needing more, trying to make it last forever.

The storm had died to a steady pelting of rain on the shingled roof as they lay entwined on the narrow sofa. Jeff's hand stroked Amelia's face, and his eyes were gentle with adoration yet dark with need.

He said softly, "I don't want you to be sorry."

Sorry. Oh, yes, she should be feeling a great many regrets, doubts and anxieties. This wasn't 1992—it was 1870. She could be marked for life, an outcast with whom no decent man would associate. She could get pregnant. She, who did not even exist in this time, could actually bear the child of this man who had no future. Yes, she had taken terrible chances. Yes, by all common sense she had made a dreadful mistake and should be very sorry. The old Amelia would have worried about those things. The Amelia who had found love in a place beyond time didn't care at all.

She caught his fingers near her lips and looked at him with joy that made all attempts at self-expression seem feeble. "Oh, Jeff," she whispered, "how can I be sorry? Don't you know that whatever happens—" her fingers tightened on his convulsively "—I will live on this moment forever?"

His arm tightened around her as he rested his head against the arm of the sofa, bringing their joined hands to his lips. "I always thought I was so good with words," he said. "But everything I want to say to you now sounds so small. I wish... God, Amy. I wish everything was different."

Her voice was a little choked as she answered, "So do I."

He shifted his weight so that he was above her, his hands holding her face and his gaze intensely fastened on her. "I'm not going to leave you," he said. "I promise you that."

Amelia closed her eyes and lifted her arms, drawing him down to her again, but she said nothing. She knew he'd made a promise he wouldn't be able to keep.

They made love again with slow, breath-suspending sweetness—touching...memorizing. The sound of the rain died and dusk crept through the cracks of the shutters while they held each other in silence, letting the world, like the rain, fade away without them.

At last Jeff reminded, "The others will be worried about us."

After a long moment, Amelia nodded. She had known it was only an interlude. Nothing could stop the passage of time. Endings were inevitable. She only wished this one hadn't come so soon.

She moved away from him and began to dress, wincing as the cold, wet fabric touched her skin, withdrawing the last of the warmth he had given her. When the last button was fastened and her damp skirts tied, Jeff was dressed, too. They looked at each other for a long moment.

"Tell them you waited out the storm in the summerhouse," he said. "I'll follow in a few minutes and say I found shelter in one of the empty cabins in the village."

Amelia nodded. And so came the onset of reality. Deception, lies, embarrassment... Things were no less complicated in this time, after all. It was simply that the lines were drawn more clearly. And today she had stepped over a line that could bring nothing but confusion and heartache for both of them.

She turned to leave, but Jeff caught her shoulders gently, turning her to him. "This is not the end, Amy," he said softly. "I just need some time to think."

"I'm not sorry," she whispered.

He drew her to him and kissed her tenderly, thoroughly, and with a lingering sweetness that made her throat sting with tears. "It's not the end," he repeated.

She left the summerhouse with the taste of his kiss on her lips and the warmth of his love inside her heart; and for a time, she almost believed him.

ELEVEN

The next morning dawned clear and sun-washed. After breakfast Amelia gathered up gloves, shears and a big basket, and joined Martha Craig in the west garden.

"The most important thing," Martha lectured her with the cheerful confidence of one who is utterly immersed in her subject, "is not to let the blossom wither on the stem—even the bulbs. Cut the flower but leave the green for growth. What a pity," she said, pinching off a zinnia whose petals had been blasted by the wind. "These poor things would have bloomed another week. Of course it's early yet. We may have another flowering."

Amelia knelt to clip a pale yellow gladiolus whose stem was bent in half and whose delicate blossoms were sprinkled with mud. "No wonder your gardens are so beautiful. You take such good care of them."

Martha Craig beamed with gratification. "Well, it does require diligence. But I always say that the only difference between the barbarism and civilization is a garden, and it's worth the effort."

For a moment Amelia just stared at her, shaken by an eerie echo from the past—a woman called Karen, pausing at the top of the stairs a century later and quoting those very words. She smiled weakly at Martha and placed the gladiolus in the basket with the others she had gathered.

Martha Craig nodded approvingly. "Those will look really nice in that vase in the front room. Why, Jeffrey, there you are. We missed you at breakfast."

The sound of his name caused Amelia's pulse to skip, and when she looked up, the sight of him flooded her whole body with pleasure. He came toward them with his hat in hand and his hair tousled by the wind, in riding boots and an open coat. Amelia felt a surge of possessive pride as she looked at him, mixed with the achingly sweet memory of sensations so vivid she could almost taste them.

He kissed his mother's cheek, but his smile was for Amelia. Her face flooded with radiance from nothing more than that smile, and she looked away quickly, absently clipping another gladiolus.

"I was out early this morning," Jeff said. "The river is up but I don't think it will overflow, and if this weather holds, the water in the fields should go down by tomorrow. I didn't see any serious damage."

"Well, wasn't that thoughtful of you to save Elliot the trouble? He's seeing Laura off at the ferry, but I know he felt bad about not checking on things himself. You're a good brother, Jeffrey."

"It's my land, too, Mother," he reminded her gently.

"Why, of course it is. Oh, no, dear. Not that one—it hasn't even bloomed yet."

Amelia stopped with her shears only a fraction away from closing about the stem of an unfurled blossom. Embarrassed by her inattentiveness, she murmured,

"Sorry." She started to get to her feet. "Maybe I'd better—"

Jeff spoke to her. "I came to tell you, Mother, that Professor Kane was looking for you. Something about that clothes-washing contraption he was working on?"

Martha Craig giggled. "Can you imagine? The dear man is always coming up with these outrageous ideas to make life easier, but frankly," she confided to Amelia, "they only make things more complicated. The old ways are always the best, or they wouldn't be old, would they? Not, of course, that I'd hurt his feelings for the world after he tries so hard. Well, excuse me, my dears. I'd best go see how I can help him." And she bustled away.

"A washing machine? I know that hasn't been invented yet. She should be glad to have it."

"Looks impractical to me," Jeff replied absently. "From what I can tell, it's going to take two strong men and a mule to run the thing."

Amelia laughed softly. "I guess so, without electricity. I think Professor Kane is a little ahead of his time."

Jeff knelt beside her. "Amy," he said, "I want you to marry me."

For a moment Amelia thought she mustn't have heard him correctly. The shears slipped from her numb fingers and she stared at him. His expression was watchful and serious.

He picked up the fallen shears and politely offered them to her. When she made no move to take them, he tucked them into her basket and took her hand and lifted her to her feet. He said, "I know what you're going to say."

At last she found her voice. "That's good. Because I don't."

Marriage. Had he said *marriage?* No man had ever proposed to her, not in all her twenty-nine years. Marriage . . . to Jeff, the only man she had ever loved; the man who understood her and strengthened the parts of her that were weak; the one man who, of all those who lived or ever would live, was meant to belong to her, and she to him.

Marriage. To Jeff, who had lived and died a hundred years before she was born, whose destiny was already written and did not include her . . .

Her head was spinning; in the space of a second her spirits plummeted from unreasoning joy to despair. She looked at Jeff helplessly. "Why?"

He smiled. "I knew you were going to say that. And do you really have to ask?"

She pulled her hand away. "Oh, Jeff, no," she said softly. Astonished, she struggled to find the words. "No, you don't understand. Just because we— Because I—" She gestured toward the summerhouse, and the memories that rushed forward only clouded her brain, making it harder to state the refusal that she knew was necessary. "I know that—in your time, marriage is the only honorable thing to do, but—"

Impatiently he shook his head. "It has nothing to do with my 'time,' as you call it, or honor, or obligation, if that's what you're thinking. For God's sake, Amy, do you think you're the first woman I've—"

He broke off, but the words didn't hurt her as he probably had been afraid they might. Seeing the lack of accusation in her eyes, Jeff's expression softened.

He took her arm and led her over to a bench in the sun, and sat beside her.

He held her hands in both of his and spoke with quiet conviction. "I have lived my life from day to day," he said, "never caring about the future because nobody ever promised me tomorrow. I turned my back on my family, I walked away from the country I'd fought to preserve. I never cared about anything, Amy, because I never had anything to lose. I didn't know that—one day, there would be you."

He lowered his gaze briefly, and his fingers tightened on hers. "Don't you see?" he said huskily. "You've made me feel alive for the first time. You've given me back things I thought I'd lost forever. You've made me care again. You're in my blood, inside my head, and I can't get you out. You're the only woman," he finished quietly, "I can ever imagine spending the rest of my life with. And I knew that long before yesterday."

Every instinct, every emotion Amelia possessed, demanded that she fling her arms around him and say, *Yes*. But how could she do that? How *could* she?

She looked at him in misery and despair. "How can I marry you? I don't even belong here. I haven't even been *born* yet. Don't you understand that? I have no life here, no place—"

"You *are* here." His interruption was calm and firm; his gaze, steady. "You can't deny that. Whatever else you claim, you can't argue that truth. Your life is here, Amy, in this time and this place, and nothing is going to change that. I'm asking you now to spend that life with me."

How clear it was when he said it: She couldn't go home again. The memories of the life she'd once had were growing distant, and all that was left to her was the life she made for herself now. With Jeff. Of course, it had to be with Jeff. But how *could* it be?

She released a broken breath. "I want that, Jeff. More than anything else in the world."

His hands tightened on hers. "I told you yesterday I had nothing to offer you. It's true, and it's tormented me more than you can know. But with you, Amy, I can make something for us. This island—this plantation—it's mine. Maybe it shouldn't be, maybe I don't deserve it, but my father never changed his will and I inherited everything when he died. I gave it up willingly and I can take it back. We can have a home here, if you want."

"You—would do that to Elliot?"

He shook his head. "I always intended to divide the place up equally among the three of us. Benjamin wants to be a big-city lawyer and he's not interested; I've just never bothered to claim my share before. I never had a reason to. Now I do."

Was that the reason for the veiled hostility she had sensed between Elliot and Jeff? Was Elliot afraid, perhaps, that his brother might one day want to claim more than a share? And could she live, knowing that she had been the cause of an open break between the brothers?

Jeff's voice was low as he went on, "I know it's not much of a life, married to a fugitive, bound to this island, but one day—"

"I love this island," she said swiftly. "I love the house, and the gardens and your family. And I could happily spend the rest of my life here, but— Oh, Jeff!'' She couldn't keep the despair at bay any longer.

She pulled her hands away and stood. "Don't you see it can't be?" she cried. "History has already been written and I can't change it! I've tried—God knows I've tried—but in ten days you're going to leave this place a hunted criminal and never be heard from again!"

She saw the expression that crossed his face and she couldn't bear to look at it. She turned away, hugging her elbows, keeping her neck stubbornly straight despite the fact that everything inside her was breaking apart.

Jeff got up and closed his hands on her shoulders. For the first time he didn't argue with her, but quietly asked, "Does history say you didn't come with me?"

With soaring hope, she turned to him, on fire with the possibilities—and then cold practicality crept in.

A wanted man, running for his life . . . She had said it before, half jokingly: All he needed was a clumsy, incompetent twentieth-century woman slowing him down. History did not say *what* had become of him. Had he lived his life in quiet seclusion someplace in Canada or Mexico? Had he died on the trail of fever or wounds, alone and unmourned? Or had he been captured and hanged in some anonymous little town because a woman made a stupid mistake?

Amelia took a breath, and the next words she spoke were the cruelest and most difficult she had ever had to form. "History doesn't say," she replied, "whether you lived or died. I can't be responsible for your death, Jeff."

She saw the muscles of his jaw clench, and he lowered his gaze. He said nothing.

She gripped his arms urgently. "Jeff, I can't even ride a horse, much less drive a team or build a campfire or find water or do any of those other things frontier women are supposed to do. I'd get sick or hurt or do something stupid to draw attention to you. You'd be worried about me when you should be worrying about yourself. You'd be trying to take care of me when you should be concentrating on getting away. I don't—I don't know how I'm going to live without you..." There, for the first time, her voice broke. "But I can't go with you."

He looked up at her. She expected anger, denial, frustration or even contempt. The quiet determination she saw there surprised her.

"Maybe *you* can't change history," he told her, "but *I* can. I'm the person involved, and I swear to you, Amy, I am not leaving you."

She wanted to sink into his arms, to close her eyes and believe in that promise, to hold on to it with her last breath. But she made her hands loosen their fierce grip on his arms, pressing them together in front of her as though by that act she could hold her emotions inside. She said, "I love you, Jeff."

He smiled faintly, and touched her cheek. "July Fourth," he said. "That's the only way I can prove it to you, isn't it? To wait and see. I've already waited a lifetime for you. A few more days won't hurt me. But I will have my answer."

She prayed, with all her might, that somehow it could be the answer he wanted.

* * *

The days marched relentlessly forward. Only two days remained until the Fourth of July.

Amelia made plans, then discarded them as worthless. She formulated half a dozen theories in her head, but how could she know which one was correct—if any? She had spent her life perfecting the art of being prepared for any contingency and now, in the most important crisis she would ever know, she was prepared for nothing.

There were so many possibilities. Would Sam Calvert's shooting be accidental or deliberate? Would it be in self-defense or cold blood? And Jeffrey's accusation... A case of mistaken identity? Or a deliberate setup—by Elliot, for example, who had a great deal more to gain than to lose by Jeff's flight from the island?

Over and over she asked herself, *What can I do? What can I do?* Could she warn Sam Calvert, try to get him off the island? Dismantle all the weapons in the house? No one would believe her warnings. Probably she would be regarded as a lunatic and sent away, where she could be no help at all. And what good would destroying the weapons do? For all she knew, the killer wasn't from the house at all, but an intruder who crept in under cover of night armed for plunder.

As desperately as she tried, she could find no way to prevent what was destined to happen to Sam Calvert. But Jeff... Why was the possibility of losing him more real, more distressing, than a man's death?

Go with him. Repeatedly that insidious little voice returned to torment her. No one had ever said he left alone. No historical absolute prevented her from going. She couldn't be *certain* that her presence would

harm him or hamper his escape in any way, and she
wanted to believe so badly that she wouldn't have to
lose him that sometimes she almost convinced herself
it was possible.

And then from the euphoria of possibilities she
would swing to the depths of reality. No, she didn't
know for certain what would happen if she went with
him. But if he was killed or captured, would she ever
be able to convince herself it wasn't her fault? Could
she sacrifice his one chance for escape for a few more
days with him? As desperately as she needed him,
could she be that selfish?

Amelia had never considered herself particularly
courageous, and Jeff was her only anchor in this alien
world. Without him she would be lost. How could she
ever find the strength to let him go?

Above and beyond the inner tumult that besieged
her in those last days was the fact that there wasn't
another opportunity for Jeff and her to be alone. She
lay in bed twisting and turning with sleeplessness,
thinking she could get through the nights if only Jeff
were beside her... but not daring to wake Abigail by
slipping from her room and into Jeff's. Every moment of her days was accounted for, as was Jeff's. If
they walked in the garden, someone was always near.
If they went for a drive by the river, someone volunteered to accompany them. If they planned a private
picnic, it turned into an elaborate party for six or
more. Under other circumstances it might have been
amusing; sometimes Amelia even wondered if this
were not Jeff's subtle way of showing her that if they
ever intended to have any privacy again, marriage was
the only solution. He seemed patiently amused by the

entire situation, but then he didn't know—or believe—how quickly their time together was running out.

And there was a part of Amelia that insisted this was for the best, that assured her their parting would be much less painful if she could put some distance between them beforehand. That was a fine theory and it would have worked, had not Amelia's heart already been so hopelessly entangled.

Time moved on, and Amelia was no closer to solving the mystery or dealing with the consequences than she'd been on the first day she walked into this house. She busied herself with the routine of daily living, trying not to think how quickly time was running out.

"There," she said, and stepped back from the window, hammer in hand, to survey her handiwork. "My contribution to civilization as we will one day know it."

She had begged a bolt of mosquito netting from Martha Craig's attic and had spent the afternoon tacking it over the downstairs windows. By stretching it taut over the window frames and using many small nails, she had created screens of a sort, and they didn't look half as bad as she had expected.

"Why, it's really rather pretty," Abigail commented in surprise. "This net softens the whole room and I'll bet it'll help keep the sun out, too."

"They'll keep the bugs out. That's the important thing."

"You surely do know how to do some interesting things." There was an admiring note in Abigail's voice as she watched Amelia return the hammer to the wooden toolbox she had sneaked out of the barn.

Amelia managed a smile. "Not really." She didn't know how to save the man she loved from his own fate. And what good was anything else when she was helpless regarding the most important element in her life?

Abigail handed her the cloth bag of nails, and Amelia stored it in the toolbox. "There. I'd better get this back before anyone misses it."

Abigail hesitated. There was a peculiar, half worried, half reluctant expression on her face, and she said, "Amelia— Could I talk to you about something?"

Amelia put the toolbox down. "Sure." The lowering of Abigail's voice, combined with an anxious biting of her lip, suggested a secret. She had a sinking feeling that secret might have something to do with Jeff.

She was therefore surprised, and relieved, when Abigail went on, "I shouldn't bother you with this, except I don't know who else to tell. It's just that— This morning, Sam and I were walking in the garden. We weren't *really* walking," she hastened to explain. "We just happened upon one another. And Sam was talking, as he does sometimes, about some kind of plan he has to make some money, and what he was going to do afterward and..." She blushed. "I'm afraid some of his plans might have included me. Which is all to the good, of course," she added quickly, "as far as I'm concerned, except that just then Colonel Talbot came up, and saw us smiling together and—I'm afraid he misunderstood. He was dreadfully angry, and all but came to blows with Sam and— Oh, Amelia, I'm afraid he's going to say something to Mama! There would be all sorts of trouble if he did. Mama might even be forced to ask the Calverts to leave. I just don't know what to do!''

Amelia said, half to herself, ''Maybe it would be best if she did.'' That would be one sure way to see that Sam Calvert was kept safe. If Sam Calvert weren't here he couldn't be shot, and Jeff couldn't be accused. Maybe *she* should be the one to report to Mrs. Craig about Abigail's infatuation. Maybe—

And suddenly it all clicked into place for her. ''Colonel Talbot,'' she said softly. She looked up at Abigail slowly, hardly daring to believe the obvious truth that was unfolding before her. ''Of course. He hates Sam Calvert. Even if he didn't want to marry you, his Southern honor would demand that he protect you from a man like Calvert. And he was a soldier. He's still fighting that war in a lot of ways. He wouldn't hesitate to—''

Abigail looked confused. ''What on earth are you talking about? All I said was—''

''It makes perfect sense.'' And it was so obvious, so beautifully apparent, that Amelia didn't even feel excitement at the discovery; merely a weakening relief. ''I should have known before.'' She had done it. She, who had arrived for a mystery weekend with nothing but hopeless incompetence at mystery solving, had just found the solution to a real life-and-death mystery. She couldn't even begin to appreciate the implications yet.

Abigail broke in impatiently, ''I don't have the first idea what you're talking about. What I want to know is whether I should go to Mama first, and explain what happened, or—''

And then Amelia heard something that froze her blood, that drowned out Abigail's words, that pushed all thoughts of Colonel Talbot and Sam Calvert from her head.

The sound in fact had been in the background for a long time—faint, indistinct, vaguely worrisome. In her preoccupation, she hadn't even noticed. And even as the sound became clearer, it was so alien, so completely unexpected, that it took a moment for Amelia to recognize it. She flung up her hand for silence, hissing, "Listen!"

Someone whistling passed close to the window, and there was no mistaking the notes of the tune this time. Amelia, rooted to the spot, with even her heartbeat suspended, stood and listened.

Abigail, looking startled and confused, said, "I don't understand—"

"That song! Do you hear it?"

"Well, yes, but—"

Amelia flew to the window. The gauzy mosquito netting revealed nothing but a view of the tree-lined drive, yet the whistling continued, growing more distant as it rounded the corner of the house. Not a mistake. Not imagination. The song was "Hey Jude." Without a thought or a backward glance at a shocked Abigail, she fled from the room.

Catching up her skirt with one hand and clinging to the rail with the other, she propelled herself down the long flight of steps, following the direction of the sound around the house. She couldn't hear anything anymore over the pounding of her heart. But she had heard it. She had heard a twentieth-century song in nineteenth-century South Carolina. *She had not imagined it.* Not this time. Not the first time. And that could only mean that someone here besides herself was from the twentieth century.... Or perhaps everyone was. Perhaps none of it had been real from the beginning—just a long, hideous practical joke; a game, an elaborate masquerade.... And whoever was responsible for it all was now just steps away.

She stopped at the entrance to the west garden, gasping for breath. Frantically she looked around. But she heard and saw nothing. It had stopped. *It had stopped....*

She wanted to throw something or hit something or stand in the middle of the yard and demand at the top of her lungs that the perpetrator of the ugly joke step forward. How could she have been so close, only to miss finding out?

And then she heard it again, distant and faint, but definitely whistling. Notes that sounded random at first and, as she moved closer, slowly began to form a melody. A very familiar melody.

Moving as quickly as she could, she followed the whistling to the barn. There she paused, clutching the edge of the open door, and she couldn't seem to make herself go farther. The whistling was clear now—a sweet, true rendering of the melancholy tune. On the other side of that door was a person who remembered "Hey Jude," a person who was a connection to the life she thought she had lost forever. An innocent time-traveler, like herself? Or the final, indisputable proof that everything she had endured these past weeks was nothing more than a hoax—the cruel manifestation of a twisted mind.

The moment she walked through that door everything would be changed. For better or worse, her world would be turned upside down once again. Just when she had begun to adjust to the new world in which she had been deposited, just as she had begun to accept her fate, everything would be torn asunder. She almost thought it would be better to walk away and pretend she'd never heard anything at all.

But she couldn't do that. Slowly, her muscles resisting with every step, she pulled herself around the door and onto the threshold of the barn.

It took a moment for her eyes to adjust to the dimness. She made out the shadow of a man, standing with his back to her, reaching overhead to secure the latch of a bin. He was still whistling, softly and absently.

And then he turned around to her and smiled.

"Jeff!" she gasped.

TWELVE

"You bastard!" she screamed hoarsely.

Amelia launched herself at him, her fists flailing, blind with the red-hot rage of betrayal. "You knew! All this time—you lied to me! It was you all along! You knew what this was doing to me and you wouldn't help—you wouldn't even believe me—and you knew it. All the time you knew because it was *you!*"

She beat him with her fists. When he tried to catch her hands she twisted away and clawed his arms, screaming, "You *lied!* You let me go on—let me think I was losing my mind—you let me fall in love with you! Oh, God, Jeff. It was you!"

"Stop it!" He caught her arms at last, close to her chest, and he shook her fiercely. "Stop it this minute, do you hear me?"

She let herself go limp, not because he commanded it, but because it was impossible to sustain such a high, burning level of emotion for a moment longer.

She pulled her arms away and stepped back, looking up at him coldly through the veil of her hair. But she didn't feel cold; she felt destroyed. And when she looked at him—her Jeff, so familiar, so strong, so sure in the midst of all the things she'd been unsure about—all she could think was, *It can't be. Don't let it be.... Not Jeff. Please, not Jeff.*

But she said in a cracking voice, "I guess you thought you were pretty clever. But it's over now. All it takes is one mistake."

There was nothing in his face but confusion, tinged with anger. "What mistake? Amy, what are you talking about?"

"For God's sake, Jeff, don't play games with me! Not now!" She didn't want to fight with him, but how could he make her stand here and prove herself to him after everything else he had put her through? "That song!" She practically spat the words at him.

"What song?" His anger was replaced by concern as he took a step toward her. "Amy are you all right? What happened to put you in such a state?"

She stepped back, violently swiping her hair away from her face. "What song?" Her voice was grating. "The one you were whistling! Or didn't you even realize you were doing it! A song that wasn't even *written* until the last part of the twentieth century! Do you want to explain that to me? Do you, Jeff?"

He hesitated. Then he said, with nothing but innocence in his voice, "Do you mean 'Hey Jude'?"

Whatever hope, frail though it may have been, that she was wrong—that she had misunderstood or misinterpreted or that there was some safe, reasonable and perfectly harmless explanation—was gone. Everything was gone. It was finished.

"Yes," she said dully. "'Hey Jude.' By the Beatles. Nineteen seventies, I think. Or late sixties. But you know that."

She forced her eyes to focus on him, and it was as though she were seeing him for the first time. So handsome, so strong, so perfectly in character in the worn butternut coat with tiny specks of chaff clinging to his hair. Smelling of leather and cigar smoke. Looking like Jeff, the man she had given her heart to. And then she discovered something odd. Her heart, once given, wasn't easily retrieved. For there was a part of her, deep inside and in spite of all else, that still loved him, and always would.

It required almost more strength than she possessed to inquire, with no emotion at all, "So, what is it? You're from the twentieth century, obviously. You probably heard the song on the radio just like I did. When? A month ago? A year ago? Or only yesterday? Did you travel through time, too, Jeff? Or has the whole thing just been a stage set, a joke that everyone is in on but me?"

He was silent for a long time. He looked at her with such intensity that she should have known. How many times had she seen that look on his face when he was trying to believe her, trying to understand even when he couldn't believe? That was the look she had first fallen in love with.

Then he said calmly, "Amelia, I don't know what you're talking about. It's an old song, a folk song. I've heard it all my life."

She almost smiled. "So now you're telling me that the Beatles were ripping off century-old folk songs from the barrier islands of South Carolina. Don't, Jeff. Just please, don't."

"No," he replied slowly. "I'm telling you that I first heard that song when I was a boy and I never thought anything odd about it. But if you say that it wasn't even written until a hundred years from now..."

But she asked, "Where? Where did you hear the song?"

He replied simply, "From Professor Kane."

She caught up her skirts and turned, not even certain where she was going. It was Jeff who took her arm and led her across the yard, behind the stables, beyond a windbreak of sapling pines to Professor Kane's workshop.

She had a dim impression of clutter, the smell of dust and oil, workbenches scattered with misshapen pieces of metal, scraps of wood and crockery jars filled with strange-smelling chemicals. And books. Books of all sorts, lying open on the workbenches, piled knee-high on the floor, lining the wall shelves almost to the ceiling. The professor himself was sitting on a high stool at a bench by the window, squinting over a snippet of wire he was trying to thread into something that looked like a small wheel.

He said, without looking up, "Well, now. I wondered when you young folks was going to come visit."

Amelia thought, *No. It's not possible.* But she looked around and her heart began to beat a little faster, though she couldn't say exactly why. *Possible...*

Jeff said, "Amelia was interested in that song you taught us when we were little. 'Hey Jude.'"

The professor grunted. "Gears," he said, twisting the wire through a small hole in the wheel. "Simplest thing in the world. With them, you get the job done. Without them, you don't."

Amelia took a step forward. She drew a breath. She said, "Do you know the Beatles?"

He didn't look up. "Pesky little critters."

No, she thought. *It can't be. This is crazy, this is foolish....* But if it wasn't Jeff who held the answer, someone did. Jeff had brought her here. Professor Kane was his only defense. She wanted to believe in Jeff.

She took another step forward. She said carefully, "General Motors?"

He answered, "Make a fine machine."

Her heart pounded in her chest with such force that for a moment she was actually dizzy. And then her mind was racing. It could have been a mistake, a lucky guess. Motors. Machine. She had made one ghastly, agonizing mistake with Jeff—she was sure of that now—and she couldn't go through it again. She wanted it to be true, she needed it to be true, but she had to be sure. She had to think. *Think.*

"Do you remember—" she swallowed "—ball-point pens and quartz watches and disposable diapers?"

He chuckled, still concentrating on his work. "Now, missy, what use would I have for junk like that? I do just fine with what I have."

Please...

She said breathlessly, "Telephones?"

"Damn nuisance. Somebody should put a word in Mr. Bell's ear on that subject."

Yes... oh, yes...

She could sense Jeff behind her, watching with alert interest, but she concentrated fiercely. No coincidences, no mistakes. She had to be so careful....

Then she asked, "Who was the fortieth president of the United States?"

He frowned a little over his work. "Why, I'm not sure I know. Would that be before Nixon?"

She took another hesitant, fumbling step toward him. Her voice was barely above a hoarse whisper. "Do you know—Captain James T. Kirk?"

He put down the small wheel he was working on and turned to look at her. His eyes were friendly and unsurprised. "Not personally, of course. Only by reputation."

He stood, wiping his hands on his rumpled pants legs as he added, "Commander, USS *Enterprise*." Then he smiled. "Welcome aboard."

Amelia closed her eyes and let the tears of overwhelming joy trickle down her cheeks. Home. That was all she could think. *Home*.

She never knew how she kept herself from breaking into sobs of laughter. But somehow she was in Jeff's arms, just holding him, just pressing her face against his chest and holding him. Then she hugged the rumpled figure of Professor Kane, and then she put her arms around both of them and smiled through her tears.

Professor Kane cleared off a chair for her and one for himself, and they sat facing each other. Jeff sat on the edge of a table a little behind her, his hand resting lightly on her shoulder. There were so many questions she wanted to ask that for a long time she didn't know where to begin.

At last she spoke. "Did you— Did you know about me?"

He made no attempt to avoid her gaze. "I suspected, from the first night. But I didn't want to know. It wouldn't have done either one of us any good."

Amelia wanted to protest, to argue with him. If only she had known she wasn't alone in those first frantic days... If only she'd been able to prove to herself and everyone else that she wasn't insane... But then she thought she understood what the professor meant. If she had known she had an ally, a companion from her own time, would she have made quite the same effort to adjust to this time? Wouldn't it have been harder, in the end, to be constantly reminded of what she had lost?

Jeff's hand tightened briefly on her shoulder. "I think I understand why you were so upset when you thought I'd deceived you. I should have put it all together sooner."

Filled with remorse, Amelia turned her cheek to his fingers, nuzzling them briefly. "No. I should have. I'm sorry, Jeff."

The professor looked at Jeff, then at her. "So he knows?"

Amelia nodded. More of the questions came tumbling forth. "It was the sundial, wasn't it?"

"Not the sundial itself, but the area around it. It's kind of a natural time channel. My guess is there are quite a few of them around the world. We just haven't discovered what they are yet."

"When did you leave?"

He smiled. "Nineteen seventy-three. I was a hotshot engineer with an interest in history. I was working with the developers of the beach project and made a point of going to see the old house. When the sundial started acting up, well, naturally, thinking of myself as some kind of expert in physics, I had to check it out. I walked right into it, and ended up in 1853.''

"Then you know," Amelia said urgently, "about Sam Calvert and what's going to happen here on the Fourth of July."

His face grew sober, and he wouldn't look at Jeff. "I know."

Amelia felt Jeff tense behind her. "But it can be changed," she insisted. "I know that now. I know—"

But Professor Kane interrupted: "While I was working on the beach project I read everything I could on this land. I knew the Civil War was coming—I didn't expect to be able to stop it. I knew young Jeff here, who I'd practically raised from a pup, was going to run off and join up. I couldn't stop him. I knew his pa was going to grieve himself to death—and he was a friend of mine, a good friend. I knew Jeff was going to get in bad trouble when he went west, and all I could do was stand back and watch it happen. After a while it got to where the only thing I could do was just try to forget what I knew. 'Cause there wasn't a thing in this world I could do about any of it.''

Jeff got up and crossed to the window, where a fly buzzed noisily against the pane. There he stood, quietly looking out. And Amelia clenched her fists, refusing to accept the professor's grim belief in the inevitability of history. She had come too far, and learned too much, to accept defeat so easily now.

"I couldn't live like that," she murmured.

"Sure you could. You're going to have to," the professor said.

A month ago, perhaps. But not now. She had too much to fight for.

And she would have told him so, but just then the professor—though he wasn't really a professor but an ordinary engineer from the twentieth-century—asked, "What year was it when you left?"

She knew he was trying to distract her from what he believed was the hopelessness of the fate that awaited Jeff. "It was July third, 1992," she replied dully.

He nodded. "The hundred-twenty-two-year cycle." Then he frowned. "But you should have arrived on the same day you left. You were early by three weeks. What happened?"

She explained to him, as best she could remember, what happened. When she was finished, he nodded.

"That was it, then. You tried to fight it, you ran, and that threw the timing off. If you'd let it pull you in, like I did, you would have arrived on July third, to the minute of when you left—minus a hundred-twenty-two years, of course."

Then he wanted to know what had changed in the years he had been gone, what the world had become in 1992. If he was still trying, in his subtle way, to distract her, the technique worked. She told him about the space shuttle and personal computers and cable TV, and though he seemed disappointed that men weren't building cities on the moon, he was fascinated by the technological revolution.

He couldn't ask enough questions—questions that covered everything from history, politics and the stock market to movies, TV and cars. And the more he asked, the more Amelia talked. Jeff listened, occasionally casting them looks of astonishment or curiosity, but never interrupted. He stood by the window, his hands clasped behind his back and his gaze, more often than not, was directed outside.

At last Professor Kane settled back, rummaging among the scraps of paper and discarded books for a pipe, which he filled and lit, shaking his head. "Wonders on top of wonders. Kind of makes me wish I could have stayed to see it. Not that I'd much like it, from what you've said. It sounds like the kind of place you might like to visit, but who'd want to live there?"

"I would," Amelia replied, and she couldn't prevent sadness from shading her voice.

The professor lit his pipe, regarding her soberly. "I can't say I don't understand how you feel, miss. I spent fifteen years of my life figuring out how to get back, but—"

Something incredible clutched at Amelia's chest. "Do you mean—there's a way to get back?"

His matter-of-fact shrug was so understated as to be almost comical. "Well, of course. The first law of physics—for every action there is an equal and opposite reaction."

For a moment Amelia's mind balked—it was too logical to be true. The most important discovery in history and the man shrugged it off. The one thing, the only thing that Amelia had thought was so impossible she dared not even hope for it—and all he had to say about it was a dismissive, "Of course." No. He couldn't be serious. He simply couldn't be.

"But— The Sundial," she insisted frantically. "I tried it. I thought— But it didn't work. Nothing happened."

"Well, of course it didn't. The thing works in cycles, like I told you. Every hundred twenty-two years there's a period of activity when the channel opens up for a short time at what seems like random intervals—but they're not really random at all. It all follows a very definite mathematical formula, and all you have to do is plot the course. And that's what I've spent the past fifteen years doing." He smiled. "In between my inventions, of course."

"But—but if you know how to go back, why haven't you?"

He tamped his pipe with a broken piece of wood. "Well, like I said, it took a lot of years to figure it all out. It would've been a lot easier with a computer," he mused. "But anyway, by the time I had the formula down, I realized there was one important variable I was missing—the time."

Amelia looked at him blankly, and he leaned forward a little, explaining, "In order to get back to the time I started from, I'd have to know exactly when it was I left. Seconds translate into months when you go through the channel, minutes into years and hours— God knows where I'd end up. And the thing is, there's no way of telling just how far off the mark a few minutes' difference would put you. Or if there is, I haven't figured it out. I could have ended up in my own future, or a boy in my own past, and I don't think even the science-fiction writers have figured out what that would do to a fellow. Worse, I could have gone back instead of forward—to the ice age, or the Dark Ages— and I kind of preferred the devil I knew, if you know what I mean."

He settled back, sucking on his pipe. "It was just too dangerous. I didn't know, not even to an approximation, what time I left 1973. And unless you've got the exact figures—hour, minute and second—there's no way to make the formula work."

"I know what time I left," Amelia said, in a small, dull voice. She reached into her pocket and numbly removed the broken watch.

Jeff's head turned toward her sharply, and Professor Kane's eyes narrowed as he leaned forward and took the watch from her. Amelia didn't allow herself to think or hope or even imagine....

Then the professor grunted. "The electrical charge could've stopped it when you went through. If so, then you've got your exact time. Assuming," he added skeptically, "that the watch was keeping good time when it stopped."

"It's a Rolex!" she protested indignantly, and slowly the professor smiled.

"Well," he said softly, "looks like you've got your ticket home."

He began madly scribbling figures and mumbling calculations. The sun poured in the closed windows and heated up the room. Her own thoughts drifted over the possibilities.... Home. Her mother and sisters, Peggy, *Star Trek,* microwave popcorn, traffic jams, beach umbrellas.

Then the professor turned to her, his smile triumphant. "Well, here you are. The channel is going to be open again in two days, between ten and ten thirty-seven at night. You go through at exactly ten twenty-seven fifteen—not a second later or a second earlier—and it should bring you back to the same time you left. It would be as though you were never gone."

Amelia took the paper he offered her, though she could make no sense whatsoever of the scribblings that covered it. Still, the possibility he had presented was too enormous not to accept. *Just like she had never left . . .*

She looked at him hesitantly. The joy that swelled through her was so overwhelming that it robbed her of words. How do you thank a man for giving you back your life? What could she do for him, what could she give him, that would in any way compare to what he had given her?

And then she knew. "You can go with me!" she exclaimed. "Now that you know where you'll end up, now that we have a time—you don't have to stay here! You can come home with me, you've found your way out!"

He smiled, but there was a touch of sadness in the smile, and he shook his head. "I thank you very kindly, miss," he said, "but I can't do that."

"But why not? I don't understand! If it works for me, why can't you—"

He raised a gentle hand, "For one thing," he said, "I can't jump into my own future. How would I make up for all those missing years? I wouldn't have any money, or a job, or even a place to stay. I wouldn't fit in, in 1992. I don't belong there."

"You could stay with me. You could—"

He shook his head, still smiling. "For another," he went on, "I don't want to go back. I knew that long before I finished work on this formula.

"In 1973," he explained simply, "I was forty-five years old, divorced, living in a furnished apartment and eating out of take-out bags. No family, damn few friends, nothing to do on Saturday night but sit home and drink beer and feel sorry for myself. At work by eight, home by five, day after empty day..."

A small reminiscent smile crossed his face. "But here, they call me 'The Professor.' Oh, they think I'm half crazy, but I kind of like that, too. I lecture at universities and I write books that people read. I've got time—all the time in the world—to do the things I like to do. Tinker around, putting things together, testing out my little theories, reinventing things that aren't ready to be invented yet.... Every day's a challenge. And then there's Miss Martha, and the kids... They're my family. I'm always welcome here. *This* is my home now. I don't want any other."

His words sank in with quiet inevitability, and long before he finished speaking, Amelia knew how he felt.

Slowly, she returned the paper to him. "I can't go," she said.

Shock was stamped on his face. "What?"

"I can't go back," she repeated. "There's too much—I care about. Right here."

"But you've got to go! I'm an old man, it's different— But you! You've got your time. You've got the channel opening up within a matter of days.... It could have been years, you know, or another century before the conditions would have been right! You'll be the first person in history to time-travel both ways. You can tell them! You've got to go!"

She shook her head.

The shock faded to astonishment, then patient disbelief. "No, you don't understand. This is not something you get to take your time thinking about. If you don't go through that channel on the Fourth of July, it won't be open again—in this time or any other—for another hundred and twenty-two years. This is your last chance."

"Then it's my last chance," she replied calmly.

She stood, and turned toward the window. That was when she realized Jeff was no longer there.

She hurried from the workshop and across the yard. The professor was still shouting after her, but she didn't hear. After a time, she pulled up her skirts and ran.

In a few brief hours she had discovered a clue to her past, accused her lover of betrayal, found a compatriot in time travel and been offered a way home. But none of those incredible events affected her with a fraction of the emotion she experienced, knowing what Jeff must be thinking now. He thought she was leaving him. After all her begging him to stay with her, after he had promised, at the risk of his own life, not to leave her, he had seen how easily she forgot him when she was offered a way home. And that was a betrayal much more profound, much more painful, than the one she had so callously accused him of earlier.

She had been so caught up in the excitement of discovering a fellow twentieth-century man, so stunned by the possibilities he had offered her, that consideration for Jeff in the matter had faded into the background. For a time she had wanted to go back, almost believed she *could* go back, but that was understandable, wasn't it? Perhaps it had taken that moment of open possibilities to put everything in perspective. Without having been offered the choice, she might never have known what it was she really wanted. But now everything was clear, and she had *no choice*.

But Jeff didn't know that.

She looked first in the summerhouse, but he wasn't there. Her hat had slipped off her head and bobbed around her shoulders on its ribbon; she shaded her eyes against the sun and looked around, breathing hard. She thought she saw the shadow of a man rounding the corner of the path that led toward the river. She called out but he didn't look back. She started to run again.

She finally caught up with him in a sunny glade near the spot where they had picnicked that day by the river. She pushed into the clearing, gasping and disheveled, and he was standing near a big weeping-willow tree, absently plucking the leaves off a long streamer. He looked up at her and smiled. "Still running around in the sun without your hat, I see."

Amelia loosened the crumpled ribbons of the hat and let it fall to the ground. She came toward him cautiously. There was so much to say, and she didn't know where to begin. She only knew that the bleak look on his face broke her heart.

She said, "Jeff—"

"The venerable professor," he interrupted her easily. "It makes perfect sense, doesn't it? A pity we didn't figure it out sooner; you would have saved yourself a lot of heartache."

Something had changed in his tone, his attitude—No. Everything had changed. Even the way he looked at her was different—with reserve, as though she were a stranger to whom he was trying to be polite. She understood that, and forgave him.

"You believe me now, don't you?" she asked softly. "About what's going to happen?"

He let the mangled willow branch drop, and his eyes followed the movement. "There was a part of me that always believed you," he replied. "Loving you, how could I not? There were some things that were just easier not to believe. I guess now I don't have a choice."

"I'm not leaving, Jeff."

"Of course, you are. Did the professor get it all figured out? Your time?"

She nodded. "The Fourth of July, ten twenty-seven at night. He says that would put me back right back where I started."

"Amazing," he murmured. "The things in this world..." Then he looked at her, and the curve of his lips was wry. "The Fourth of July. Ironic, isn't it? It's like, one way or another, something means to send us on our separate ways."

She repeated, "I'm not leaving you, Jeff."

"Don't be crazy. This is your chance to go home. You *have to* take it."

His dismissal was so matter-of-fact that her nerves rankled with defensive anger. She strode up to him and looked him in the eye. "I love you, Jeffrey Craig," she said firmly. "I'm not leaving you. Nothing can make me leave you. Do you understand that?"

"Don't talk like a fool!"

Jeff's voice was sharp and his eyes narrowed. Beneath the veil of pain was bitterness, and that was easier to bear than the sorrow she had seen in his eyes before. "There won't be anything to leave," he insisted. "I won't even be here—that's what you've been trying to tell me for the past two weeks. Or have you changed your mind? Nothing can change history, isn't that right? What sense is there in your staying here where you don't belong?"

"Oh, Jeff, don't you see?" she cried. "*You're* the only thing that's important to me now. I traveled a hundred and twenty-two years to find you and I'm not going to lose you now! I can't go back!"

"That's crazy," he said gruffly, but his expression softened. He half lifted his hand as though to touch her, then let it drop. His jaw tightened again, and his voice roughened. "What's the point in it? What good will it do you to stay?"

She shook her head impatiently. "If you'll listen to me for just a minute, that's what I've been trying to tell you! Jeff," she persisted, "I know who it was. I know who shot Sam Calvert."

Quickly she explained about Colonel Talbot and the unlikely love triangle between Sam, Abigail and the colonel. "Abigail said they practically came to blows today," she finished urgently. "The stage has already been set. He's the only one who knows about Sam and her, and the only one with a motive—"

"What about the necklace?" Jeff interrupted.

"Maybe he did take it. Abigail said he's not as well-off as he pretends, and that would be just his idea of revenge. He half believes the necklace was bought with money stolen from the Confederacy anyway, so it would be just like him to think it was his *right* to take it."

Jeff started to shake his head, and she continued, "Or maybe the necklace is just a smoke screen. Did you ever think about that? Maybe it was never stolen at all. Maybe it was part of a cover-up to protect the colonel—blame it on a thief, instead of a crime of passion."

Jeff's expression was thoughtful. "That makes a little more sense. But still—"

"Jeff, don't you see? It has to be him! That's the only answer that makes sense! And now that we know that, we can stop it."

He looked away from her, frowning into the distance. "I'll admit," Jeff said at last, "that it's not impossible. The colonel is hotheaded enough to pull a gun, especially if he thought he was defending the honor of his intended. And there may even be something to what you said about the necklace. What I don't understand is what you think can be done about it."

"Get him off the island," Amelia insisted, "before the Fourth. That way—"

Jeff was shaking his head before she even finished. "You know I can't do that—not unless you want *me* to duel with him. What reason could I give? What makes you think he'd even listen to me?" He smiled a little. "I may be a fellow Confederate, but he's a colonel and all I ever made was lieutenant."

Amelia knew he was right. If she were cleverer, and if she had more time, perhaps they could devise some scheme.

"Then disarm him," she said. "And make sure he stays away from Sam Calvert that night. Between the two of us, that shouldn't be too hard."

"Amy," Jeff said gently, "there are a dozen guns in this house. I can't get rid of all of them, and if Talbot wants to shoot somebody, he'll find a gun." And then his brow furrowed slightly. "Except . . ."

She grasped his hand. "Except what?"

"It's a party," he said slowly. "A lot of folks will be bringing their children. Mother always locks the gun room when children are around. Of course, the guests don't keep their weapons in the gun room."

"That night they will," Amelia declared firmly. "You'll have to get Colonel Talbot's gun and lock it away—along with any others you find."

"As far as I know," Jeff murmured, "he's the only one who carries a gun. The doctor didn't come here with one, and the professor doesn't even own a hunting rifle."

"Then that's that," Amelia said. Her voice was weak with relief. "We can do it."

Jeff turned to her, taking both of her hands in his. His troubled expression was tender. "And what if we can't?" he inquired. "What if your theory is wrong? What if it's not Talbot? What if, in spite of every precaution we take, we can't change history after all?"

Amelia shook her head fiercely. "No. We *can*. We have to."

"But if the professor is right," he insisted, "if there's nothing anyone can do about the future, then it will all happen as it was written. I will have to leave here and you'll be alone. You can't take that chance, Amy," he told her, his fingers tightening on hers. "You have to go back where you belong."

Amelia drew a breath. It was amazing, how easily the words came, though until that moment she hadn't entirely thought it through. But it was as though somehow in the past few days—or the past few hours—the answer had come to her. The only possible answer. And it seemed so inevitable, she only wondered why she hadn't understood it.

She said, "All my life, I've been afraid of change, of taking chances, of—the unknown, I guess. But I've changed, Jeff. I'm still afraid, but I've found out there are some things worth taking chances on.

"If I go back," she said, and now she spoke slowly, discovering the truth as she went, "I'll be safe. I'll be back where I belong, where everything is familiar and routine and I know what to expect. But a part of me— the only part that ever meant anything—will be back here, with you, lost forever in time.

"If I stay..." And again she took a breath, meeting his eyes bravely. "Maybe you're right. Maybe we'll never see each other again. Maybe you'll leave this island and that will be the end of it. *But maybe it won't.* No one knows. I haven't read all the history books, I haven't researched the records. All I know is what I read in a cheap tourist brochure, and even Professor Kane doesn't know any more than that. At the very least, Jeff, I can stay here and help to clear your name. I *can* do that. And when it's all over, maybe you can send for me, or come back. It's a chance, the only one we've got. And don't tell me you wouldn't do the same thing in my place."

He looked at her for a long time, and his expression was unreadable. Then he said huskily, "I wouldn't be so damn stupid about it." But he drew her into his arms and held her tightly.

She wound her arms around him, feeling the expansion of his chest and the contraction of his muscles as his hands traveled the length of her back, pushing through her loosened hair, cupping her neck. And she had never been more certain of the rightness of anything than she was at that moment. Without him, she had nothing. With him, anything was possible.

"Amy, listen to me." With his fingers spread on either side of her head, he gently tilted it back. His eyes were dark, his face achingly sober. "It won't work." And when she drew a breath to protest, his fingers tightened slightly and he insisted, "No, just listen. I can't let you do this. It would be different if it were me—I can live anywhere, get used to anything, and God knows, I've done my best to prove it in my lifetime. But you... Don't you think I've seen the look in your eyes when you talk about home? Don't you think I know how much you miss it, and what all this has done to you? This time—this place—it's not yours, and it never will be. You need things I can never give you, as much as I want to. And I could never forgive myself for keeping you from what you deserve. I don't know what kind of future I'm going to have. I can't even promise to keep you safe—"

"Do any of us?" she interrupted.

He looked blank, and she insisted, "Do any of us know what kind of future we're going to have? Is there any guarantee that I would be 'safe,' as you call it, in the twentieth century? The only thing I can guarantee is that I'd only be half alive without you. The rest is up to fate."

He dropped his head, touching his forehead gently against hers. "Oh, Amy."

She looped her arms around his neck and took a step backward, looking him in the eyes. "I want to marry you, Jeff Craig."

The tenderness and the sadness in his smile filled her soul. "That simple, is it?"

She nodded seriously. "That simple. Then, no matter how far apart we are, I'll always know you belong to me."

He caressed her cheek with the back of his knuckles. "You don't need a vow to make that so."

She said, "Now."

He dropped his hand. "It will take a week to get a preacher out here."

She took both of his hands in hers, holding his gaze with her own. "I, Amelia," she said softly, "take you, Jeff, to be my wedded husband, to have and to hold, to love and to cherish, till death do us part."

For a long time there was nothing but the twittering of the birds, the distant sound of the river. Sunlight dappled his shoulders and played in his hair. Then he lifted her hand and touched it to his lips.

"I, Jeffrey," he said, "take you, Amelia, to be my wedded wife. To have and to hold, to love and to cherish, till—" And there his voice seemed to catch, and he finished softly, "death do us part."

And then Jeff smiled and looked down at their entwined fingers. "I don't have a ring for you."

Amelia pulled her hands away. "I have something for you." She reached up and unfastened her necklace, then placed it around Jeff's neck, closing the catch. Her own smile was a little tremulous. "Just to remind you of me."

He touched the small initial pendant lightly, then drew her into his arms. Together they sank to the mossy ground. And there beneath the veiled curtain of the weeping-willow tree, they made their bed.

THIRTEEN

The Fourth of July dawned hot as a steaming kettle, and overcast. Amelia got up, dressed and went downstairs. All morning she watched in dismay as the house filled with people. Dowdy matrons in dove gray, girls with flowery accents and ruffled bosoms, handsome young men and gangly teenage boys, loud-talking war veterans, children... *So much noise,* she thought. *So much confusion. Anything could happen....*

Over twenty people came to celebrate the holiday with the Craigs. There was dancing and eating and exchanging of recipes. It was like a picture postcard from the past: fiddle music and girls in bright dresses and palm fronds silhouetted against the sky; little boys chasing each other with frogs, and old people rocking on the veranda.

"It doesn't seem possible," Amelia said to Jeff. It all seemed so faraway and unreal, like a dream. "It doesn't seem possible that anything bad could happen."

He squeezed her hand. "Maybe it won't."

She looked up at him anxiously. "The guns?"

"All locked up," he assured her. "Even the colonel's. He won't miss it unless he goes looking for it, and I hope he won't have any reason to do that."

With that reassurance, Amelia was able to relax a bit. Without a gun, how could there be a shooting? Nothing could go wrong. Every possibility was covered.

Between the two of them, they never let Colonel Talbot out of their sight. But even more important, as far as Amelia was concerned, she made certain Jeff was never far from her. As long as he was with her, he couldn't be accused of a crime he didn't commit. And to her enormous relief, neither Colonel Talbot nor Jeff was approached by Sam Calvert at all. It was going to work. Everything was going perfectly.

After the feast, when all the ladies went to lie down, Amelia sneaked away and hid herself in the summerhouse. After a time Jeff joined her and they made love with the frantic abandon of the first time—or the last. Afterward, as they held each other with muscles straining and heartbeats still thundering, Jeff whispered, "Amy, you must promise me—"

But she knew what he was going to say. "No." She tightened her arms around him. "I won't go back. I won't leave you. You can't make me promise you that."

His muscles tensed. "Amy—"

"We're going to be okay," she insisted, looking into his eyes. "Don't you see that? It's working, just like we planned, and nothing is going to happen. *Nothing.* We'll get through this day and everything will be all right. You'll see."

"The day isn't over until midnight," he answered quietly. "And if you don't leave by ten twenty-seven—"

"I'm not listening to this," she said fiercely, burying her head in his shoulder.

He put his fingers under her chin and lifted her face. His gaze was sober. "Then do this," he told her softly. "Let's both—just promise each other that we'll do whatever we have to to survive."

He held her and kissed her, and that answer was enough.

Her kiss was the answer, and it was given freely. He was survival to her, and nothing else mattered at all.

Amelia, waltzing in Jeff's arms in the foyer, suddenly realized that the day was almost over. Sam Calvert was dancing with a girl in a red dress, looking as though he didn't have an enemy in the world. Colonel Talbot danced with Abigail. The sun had set and thunder rumbled in the distance, but *nothing had happened.* Everything was as it should be. History *could* be changed. They were going to make it. . . .

Amelia looked into Jeff's eyes and laughed. He must have read her thoughts because his eyes sparkled back and he whirled her around so enthusiastically that her petticoats belled.

"I know it now, Jeff," she said. "Everything's going to be all right. This is just the beginning for us. The best part of our lives." And she really meant it; she felt it through to her bones. They had survived. Nothing could separate them now.

When it was fully dark everyone began to drift to the buffet tables, filling their plates and their glasses and moving out onto the verandas for the best view of the fireworks display, which would be conducted from the marshes around the island. Jeff took Amelia's hand and nudged her through the crowd, out into the relative privacy of the yard.

"I have to help set up the illuminations," he said, leading her down the path that curved toward the back gardens. "It won't take long. I'll leave you in good hands."

Though the rain seemed to be holding off, the wind had picked up considerably, plucking at Amelia's skirts and disarranging her carefully coiffed hair. The wind had a hot, electric bite to it, and it went through Amelia with a stab of prescience she couldn't ignore. She clutched Jeff's arm anxiously. "No. I'll go with you."

"This is no job for a woman," he teased, but his voice had a tense edge to it.

"You shouldn't be alone. In case— In case something happens. I don't think it will but in case it does, I should be there—"

And then she realized where he was taking her.

Professor Kane paced back and forth along the edge of the small, ivy-covered garden. The wind whipped his coattails straight back and tangled his already unkempt hair and he looked like one of those caricatures of the mad scientist in an old movie. The lights from the house were bright enough to shed a hazy illumination over the entire square of garden, but some trick of nature seemed to have concentrated most of the light on the sundial in the background, infusing it with an almost-radiant glow.

The professor strode toward them impatiently. "About time!" he declared. "Twenty minutes. That's cutting it close, you know." He pulled out his pocket watch and squinted at it. "We've got to be exact, can't take any chances— Look! It's already beginning to open up.''

Amelia looked in horror from the sundial, which now seemed to be surrounded by a hazy, distorting aura of light, to Jeff. "No!" she gasped. The wind was stronger here, and it had lost its humid, rainy taste. It seemed to swallow up her breath. "I told you, I'm not going. You can't make me!"

Jeff's face was sober, and rock hard. "You're going,'' he said. "And the professor here is going to see that you do. If I have to tie you up and gag you senseless, you're going back home where you belong. Where you'll be safe."

She took a step backward, prepared to run if she had to, but she was still holding on to Jeff's arms, wanting to shake him. "Jeff, you're not thinking! Only a few more hours and we'll be safe! Don't you see that nothing is going to happen? We've changed it! There's no reason for me to leave! If you think I'm going to throw away the only thing I ever cared about without even knowing . . .''

A look passed between Jeff and the professor that was grave and meaningful. Jeff said, "I'm sorry, Amy, I can't take any chances. You're too important to me for that.''

He took her shoulders, holding her lightly, and his expression gentled as he said, "When a man takes a wife, he's responsible for her. I have to do what I think is best, Amy, no matter how much it hurts.''

She wrenched away from him, wild with denial, and the professor moved quickly forward, and suddenly the night was rent by the sound of a bloodcurdling scream.

Amelia froze. A flash of lightning, long and slow, illuminated Jeff's white, still face. From the house the strains of the music faltered and stopped, and above the clamor of voices came the woman's scream again, "Stop! Help me! Somebody help! Thief!"

Oh, no. Oh, God... God, no, it can't be! Don't let it be...

She felt the stiffening in Jeff's muscles as he pushed her away and started to run toward the house. Dimly she heard Professor Kane, desperation making his voice shrill as he cried, "Jeff, don't! For God's sake, don't!" And Amelia was running, too, though she never felt her feet move. She was running as though in a dream, with the wind tugging at her and her breath roaring in her ears and familiar pieces of landscape whipping by... trying to stop Jeff, trying to help him, just trying to stay with him.

They weren't moving toward the house, after all. And it should have come as no surprise to her. The sound she heard—sharp, definite, and shatteringly close—could have been a clap of thunder or the first of the fireworks, but she knew it wasn't; they both knew it wasn't.

They came into the west garden only an instant later and saw what they knew they would see and yet never had expected to see: one man crumpled against the wall, a dark stain soaking his jacket and the front of his coat; another man standing over him with a gun held limply in his hand. The man with the gun looked up, and the light from the overhead windows revealed his face too clearly, freezing the moment in shock.

Jeff spoke the name: "Elliot."

Somewhere in the background there were alarmed voices and running footsteps, windows opening and people shouting. But none of it seemed real to Amelia, none of it important. She stood and watched like a spectator at a costume drama, riveted, fascinated, but uninvolved.

Jeff moved forward and took the gun from his brother's unresisting fingers. He knelt beside the body of Sam Calvert, and touched his throat. He looked up at his brother. "He's dead."

Elliot began to babble. "I was near the door when Mrs. Calvert screamed. She'd had a headache, gone upstairs. I guess he didn't expect her. She was screaming—something about a thief climbing out her window. It took a while because I had to unlock the gun room, but I couldn't come out here unarmed.... I called out, I swear I did. I only meant to fire a warning shot but he turned— It's my house, damn it. A man has a right to protect his own house, doesn't he? I never meant to hit him. I never meant to—"

The words were choked off. Elliot's face was deathly white. He was shaking uncontrollably. Jeff reached forward and took something out of the dead man's hand. Amelia knew immediately what it was, and her heart lurched.

He went on, "I couldn't see. You've got to understand it was dark and I thought it was one of the villagers. So many people...easy to sneak in and steal something. But I wouldn't have shot him...even then I didn't mean to shoot...."

Jeff stood, the string of glittering jewels looped around his fingers. "His own stepmother," he said quietly. "He stole from his own stepmother."

Elliot grabbed for Jeff. "What am I going to do?" he demanded desperately. "Damn it, Jeff, help me! What am I—"

Amelia should have heard the sound sooner but she didn't. Of course, she didn't. A door being pushed open, voices directly overhead, a woman's scream.

"My son! You've killed my son!"

Mrs. Calvert was leaning over the gallery rail, her face grotesquely distorted and illuminated by the backwash of blazing lights from the room. Five or six people crowded in behind her and they all saw what lay below: a dead man on the ground, Elliot holding Jeff in a restraining grip, Jeff with a gun in one hand and a stolen necklace in the other.

Somebody shouted, "Hold him, Elliot!" And someone else, "Get out of my way— Got to get help!" A woman wailing, someone else sobbing, and Jeff's eyes met Amelia's in a single moment of awful understanding.

With quick, decisive movements, Jeff stuffed the gun into his belt and the necklace into his pocket. He turned and ran.

Amelia wanted to stop him; she knew she should stop him. *Don't let him go— Jeff, don't leave me—* But she couldn't stop him. She had to help him get away, far away, as fast as he could. His life depended on it.

She ran with him, and when he ducked onto a side path that led back into the gardens and away from the stables, she cried, "Jeff, no! A horse— You've got to hurry!"

He reached back and caught her hand, pulling her with him, running and stumbling, and she cried,

"Jeff, no! I can't— You have to go alone, you have to hurry! Jeff, please!"

Lightning flashed around them and a gust of hot wind pushed Amelia's skirts against her legs. She couldn't hear the sounds of pursuit; she couldn't hear the claps of thunder or the blowing of the wind; she couldn't hear anything except a low, electrical humming....

Professor Kane rushed toward them. His hair was standing straight up with an electrical charge and the sundial glistened and glowed in the background. The entire garden was lit by a white radiance. Amelia's throat was hot and dry, her skin tingled; she couldn't say anything, she could barely draw a breath.

Jeff stopped, and turned toward her. His eyes looked wild in the light, his hair tossed by the wind, his face a blur of energy and determination. "I promise," he said. He grabbed her hand and pressed it briefly, hard against the pounding of his heart. "Forever."

And suddenly he turned and ran. In four long strides he covered the distance between Amelia and the sundial. There was a shimmer, a flash of white light, and he was gone.

She didn't believe it. Even as she watched, she didn't believe it. The wind whipped around her, spikes of static electricity pulled at her skin and her hair, and there was a sound, low and keening, building in force, and vaguely she realized it was coming from her own throat.

"*No!*" she screamed, and flung herself toward the sundial.

Professor Kane grabbed her arms, pulling her back. "No! It's not your time!"

"Let me go, you fool!" She struggled with him, she kicked at him, flailed at him with her fists. "I've got to go with him! Let me go!"

"It's too late!" He held on to her with a strength that belied his frail appearance. "He's gone! You can't find him now! *It's too late!*"

"No!"

He caught both her arms, turning her toward him. He shook her, shouting, "He's lost in time! There's no way to ever find him. He may be dead, Amelia. You can't follow him! It's over! He's gone."

"No! No...God, no...." She was sobbing, staring at the sundial, but no longer fighting the professor's restraint. "No. He promised..."

He drew her close. "Your time is coming. You're going home."

Another gust of hot wind tore at her hair, and the sundial seemed to pulse and enlarge behind its veil of shimmering energy. She tried to push away from the professor, shaking her head wildly, though she no longer knew why. "No, I'm not going! I promised him! He might come back! I can't leave, I won't leave!"

There was no reason to fight, surely she knew that. There was nothing to stay here for. But this was Jeff's home, his time, the place where he belonged. There was nothing for her in the future and nothing for her in the past but memories. Still, she couldn't leave. She couldn't abandon the only thing she had left of Jeff....

The professor wound his hand around her upper arm in a grip that could have crippled, and with the other hand he opened his pocket watch. "Two minutes!" he shouted against the rising wind and the maddening, deafening, piercing hum of magnetic electricity.

She fought him, and he held on to her. She could feel the charge pulling at her, clawing at her, pressing her skirts flat, burning her skin. It was a nightmare she had lived not once, but twice, and when the professor began to drag her forward she pleaded, "Don't! Don't do this! I have to stay here, don't you see? I can help him, I can—"

Professor Kane's face was grim and unrelenting. He said, "I'm sorry, miss. I promised Jeff."

He placed his hands on her shoulders and pushed her forward, into the sundial.

FOURTEEN

"Amy!"

The voice sounded familiar, an echo from far away that had no meaning to her. Amelia fought a wave of nausea and reached out blindly to steady herself.

When her head cleared she realized she was standing in a garden. It was daytime, or early evening. Gray clouds scuttled overhead and something wet splashed on her face.... Rain. Only rain. Her hand was braced against something cold and hard—the sundial. She jerked away as though she had been burned, but it was only stone. Harmless now.

The voice called her name again and she looked around. The female figure who approached was wearing a long yellow calico dress and trying to shield her elaborate coiffure from the rain with her hands. Amelia whispered, "Peggy?"

"Where have you been? I've been looking all over! Come on." Peggy caught her arm. "They had to move inside because of the rain. Good thing I found you or you'd be soaked. This place is a maze, isn't it?"

Amelia let the other woman pull her along a few steps, then she stopped to stare. It was Peggy. It really was. Blond hair, peach lipstick, perfect tan, Giorgio perfume. *It was Peggy!*

Words and exclamations bubbled up inside Amelia and demanded to be expressed but she couldn't find her voice. She couldn't even form her thoughts.

A dream? Could it all have been a dream, from the very beginning? She could have fallen and hit her head, and everything that came after could just have been an unconscious hallucination—weeks crushed into a few seconds the way a person's life passes before one's eyes at the instant of death.... All of it—the plantation, Martha Craig's recipes, Abigail's crush on Sam Calvert, Professor Kane... Jeff. A dream. *Oh, God. Don't let it be a dream....*

And then Peggy's eyes narrowed with concern and she said, "Are you all right? You look awful. Maybe you'd better run upstairs and fix your hair. Where did you get that dress? I don't remember seeing it in the wardrobe."

Amelia looked down at the pink chintz and a breath of relief went through her. *Not a dream.* At least she had that. The memory was real. Jeff was... had been ... real.

And so was his loss.

And yet, with the awful wave of sorrow that went through her, there was also a sense of wonder, of something gained as well as lost. For a time, no matter how brief or improbable, she had known love; she had learned to fight for that love and she had grown strong with the fight. In the end she had lost, but she had no regrets. What she had known with Jeff would be with her forever, and if she had it to do all over again she wouldn't change a thing. She had known him and loved him and she would never be the same because of it; and that was worth any pain, past or future, that life might offer.

She stroked the folds of her gown and said softly, "It was Abigail's." Abigail, who had loved as unwisely as she and had lived out her life a hundred years ago. Had she been happy? Had she ever loved again? Had she missed Amelia when she was gone? Martha Craig, Benjamin, even the eccentric Professor Kane— they had been her friends, her family. They were gone now, buried for a hundred years. But she would carry their memories with her, as real as yesterday, to the end of her life.

Peggy glanced again at the dress and shrugged. "Oh, well. Just as well. Pink's a rotten color for me, anyway."

A sudden urge to blurt out everything that had happened died, fading into a wistful smile. Peggy wouldn't have believed her anyhow, and Amelia had been through all of that before.

Peggy tugged on her arm, quickening her steps as the big drops of rain came faster. "Hurry up, we're missing the best part. Everybody's all dressed up and you have to remember who you're supposed to be because they're really taking this seriously. It's a riot, Amy. You're going to love it."

Amelia felt dizzy.

They entered through the foyer just before the heavy rainfall began. Amelia had a blurred impression of familiar furnishings that were just slightly off, just slightly wrong. She tilted her head and looked up the stairs; Martha Craig's portrait was in place. It almost made her smile. The woman's vanity had come through in the end—the portrait she had approved bore very little resemblance to herself.

Peggy dragged her into the parlor where the chatter and clink of cocktail glasses combined with modern guests dressed up in old-fashioned costumes was so bizarre as to make Amelia's head swim. She swallowed hard and touched Peggy's arm. She couldn't do this. She simply couldn't.

"I have a headache," she murmured. "I think I'd better—"

"Oh, don't be a spoilsport. You'll love it. You've just *got* to meet some of these people," she added with a giggle. "They're wild. Now, remember," she warned, pulling a straight face. "Pretend."

Holding on tightly to Amelia's arm, Peggy edged through the crowd. She raised her hand and called, "Oh, Mrs. Craig." And Amelia's heart stopped.

Karen Striker, as Martha Craig, turned with a smile.

After that first jolt, it was a little easier for Amelia. She was dazed and weak, and too shocked from all that had occurred to react to much of anything. Her head whirled from the onslaught of conflicting impressions as Peggy made introduction after introduction. A skinny redhead as Mrs. Calvert. A handsome actor as her stepson. The businessman Amelia had first seen in the foyer when she checked in played Colonel Talbot, and a young man with a Wall Street haircut was Professor Kane.

Then Peggy giggled, "You'll never believe who's playing Benjamin Craig."

She introduced the handsome young parking attendant, and Amelia managed a smile.

"And last but not least..." Peggy pulled Amelia along behind her as she boldly walked up to a man who was engaged in a conversation with a group of four other guests, and tapped him on the shoulder. "Jeffrey Craig."

He turned.

His face was lean and strong, his jawline square. His eyes were emerald green. His tan was a smooth, dark golden color, and the lines on his forehead were deeper than they should have been. His body was leaner and tauter, and his hair was too long—brushing his collar in the back—and lightly peppered with gray at the temples. But other than those few irrelevant differences, he could have been Jeffrey Craig's twin.

At first she thought she was hallucinating. She heard Jeff's name and she saw what she wanted to see. And then he smiled, and it went through her like a knife.

Peggy said, "Jeffrey, I'd like you to meet my dear friend, Amelia." She gave Amelia a nudge in the ribs. "Say hello, Amy."

Amelia just stared.

Jeffrey Craig bowed slightly, smiling. "Miss Amelia and I have already met," he said.

That voice. *That voice.* As smooth as silk, as rich as cream.... Amelia actually saw spots before her eyes, and the fist that was squeezing her heart tightened until she thought her entire chest would burst. It was him. *It was Jeff.* But how could it be?

Peggy lifted her eyebrows. "Well, well," she murmured, glancing at Amelia. "Been holding out on me, have you?"

Jeff's eyes never left hers. She wanted to look away, she *needed* to look away, but she couldn't. He said smoothly, "As a matter of fact, I've been waiting for you. I was getting worried."

Jeff! She wanted to shout the name; to fling her arms around him, to grip him by the shoulders and stare into his eyes and drink him in.... It was Jeff; but it couldn't be Jeff. *It couldn't be.*

Jeff glanced at Peggy. "I wonder if you'd excuse us for a minute? There's something I want to show Amelia."

Amelia saw the amazed and appreciative look in Peggy's eyes as the man who called himself Jeffrey Craig took Amelia's arm. She didn't have the strength to resist as he led her through the crowd and out into the foyer. She couldn't breathe, she couldn't take her eyes off him, and she held on to sanity with a desperate grip. It was bad enough to have had her world upended once, but twice....

Yet that was exactly why she couldn't squelch the hope that leaped inside her. She had known the impossible once; she had seen the rules of logic and reason shattered and had emerged stronger for it. She could face anything now. She could believe anything. Wasn't it conceivable that the impossible could happen twice for the sake of love? Yes, for the sake of love, anything was possible....

He pushed open the door, and they stepped onto the veranda. The rain was coming down in sheets, sealing off the rest of the world with a glassy curtain, sending a fine, cooling mist onto the veranda. Amelia walked forward and gripped the rail, turning her face up to catch the mist. He followed, standing close behind her but not touching her.

It could be a mistake. He could be an impostor, an incredible look-alike, even a descendant.... She tried to allow for those possibilities. But her heart was pounding and her thoughts were leaping with wild, incredible joy and she knew—deep in her soul she knew—that she couldn't believe that.

Then he said softly, "Amy. It's been a long time."

That voice. That beautiful voice. There was a wave of disorientation—the past and present blurred, and for a moment all she wanted to do was sink into his arms. *Jeff. Let it be Jeff....*

She turned slowly. His eyes engulfed her. His face— older, more sober, subtly changed—imprinted itself on her heart. A distant voice warned her, *Be careful....* But she paid it no heed. She lifted unsteady hands to his throat, slipping her fingers beneath his collar, and he watched her, unprotesting.

She found the chain of a necklace, and with her heart pounding in her throat, she lifted it over his collar. It was a small gold pendant with the initial *A* suspended from a chain.

"Jeff." Somehow her lips formed the words, somehow her feet took the step. Then she was in his arms, held hard against him. Then his mouth was covering hers. When they parted she was laughing and crying, and he had to hold her tightly again to ward off the onset of hysteria.

After a haze of half-formed words, frantic touches and long, searching kisses, they sat together on a wicker settee. His arm was around her, her head nestled in his shoulder, their hands tightly entwined. She could feel his heartbeat, and his breath against her hair. She managed only two coherent words: "Tell me."

He brushed a kiss against her hair. "It was the only thing I could do. I guess it started to take shape in my head that day with Professor Kane, and then, when it happened . . . I knew I had to take the chance."

She moved her head to look up at him, and he smiled. "Jeffrey Craig was never heard from again," he said. "I knew—no matter what was at stake, no matter what the history books said—I wouldn't be able to stay away from you. But you were right—if you had tried to come with me, or I had come back for you, I probably would have gotten both of us killed. This way . . . I knew if I went through the channel you would follow me, and you'd be safe. And I knew I could count on the professor to get you home. I'd hoped to have more time, so that we could go together, but I knew I couldn't count on that."

A shudder went through her hair that shook her very soul. "Jeff, the chance you took. You could have ended up anywhere, any time. You could have . . . died."

"It was the only way to make history come true," he replied simply. "Besides, I told you before—I can survive anywhere." He lifted his hands, stroking her hair away from her face. His expression was tender. "I had nothing left back there, Amy. I'd made a mess of my life and there was no chance of saving it. The only thing I had to lose was you, and I had to take a chance that, this way, I wouldn't lose you."

Amelia leaned her head against his shoulder again, limp beneath the weight of all that his words implied.

She didn't fight the knowledge, but let it flow through her—warm, sure, sweet. Jeff. He was real. He was here. That was all that mattered.

But then she had to push away again and look at him. "You're—different," she said.

His eyes crinkled at the corners, deepening with lines that hadn't been there before. "I should be. I'm seven years older."

Her gasp was a single word: "What?"

He nodded, eyes twinkling. "When I arrived the year was 1983. You wouldn't believe how much that necklace was worth by then. And the best part was that all the people who could claim it were long since dead and buried so it wasn't technically stolen...." He seemed to consider that for a moment, then shrugged. "Even if it was, there was nothing I could do about it. I had almost forgotten I had it in my pocket until I went to pay for a meal and the man wouldn't take my money—he said my coins were antique and I should stop flashing them around before I got into trouble. Anyway, between my gold pieces and the necklace and —" a slight shadow crossed his face "—Elliot's pistol, it seems I was carrying around a small fortune. By the time I invested it all..." He smiled at her. "You thought I wasn't listening when you talked about the twentieth century but I was, and thanks to you my investments turned out quite nicely. I had enough to live on and—" he nodded toward the house "—to buy this place at an estate sale and restore it."

"You—you own the plantation?" It was almost too much for her to absorb.

"Just the hotel and the surrounding acreage. That's all I wanted. All I needed to make everything the way you remembered."

"Oh . . . Jeff." Past and present, future and past—so inextricably intertwined. She couldn't begin to comprehend it now. Perhaps she never would.

There was a long silence. The rain continued to pour down and occasionally the muted sounds of voices drifted from the house; the smell of hors d'oeuvres and women's perfume, the clink of glasses. At last Amelia's scattered thoughts settled on the one thing that was closest to her memory—the past of a hundred and twenty-two years ago.

"I think I know why he did it," she said slowly. "Abigail tried to tell me but I wouldn't listen. She said Sam had a plan. He needed money to be free from his stepmother and build his own life—maybe with Abigail. So he just took what he believed was rightfully his—the necklace. And then poor Elliot . . ."

Jeff nodded soberly. "He always wanted to be a hero. To prove he could be head of the house as well as I could. He didn't have to prove anything, though. He wasn't competing with me. I wish I had told him that. Maybe things would have been different."

Amelia looked at him reluctantly. "But he let you take the blame, Jeff. All these years, you've been accused of a crime you didn't commit."

Jeff's smile was wistful. "Not really. I thought so, too, at first, and it hurt. But then I started looking up old records and it seemed Elliot *did* try to confess, but no one would believe him. Why should they? I was the renegade, the outlaw. Elliot was a respectable citizen. And of course Mrs. Calvert wouldn't let anyone believe that her own son stole the necklace. The story went out that he was shot trying to stop the thief and for a while it was a big scandal as everybody started throwing accusations back and forth. That's how we came to have a mystery worth solving this weekend.''

Mystery...weekend.... That phrase had the effect of drawing Amelia back, with whatever difficulty, to the present. And then some of the meaning of what Jeff had told her before began to sink in.

"Seven years," she said. She looked at him in amazement and confusion. "Jeff...seven years."

"It's not as bad as twenty years, or fifty," he said lightly. "Then I would have been an old man and you wouldn't want me."

"Never," she insisted, and hugged him.

His hand caressed her back. "It was hard," he admitted. "Sometimes I wondered if it would ever happen, if I was going crazy—or if I'd go crazy waiting. Once," he confessed, "I went to Richmond, and looked up your name in the phone book, and I stood outside your apartment for almost four hours...but I was afraid to knock. Superstition, maybe, but I was afraid that if I did anything to change the way we really met, something would go wrong and we'd never meet at all. Besides," he added more practically, "you wouldn't have recognized me then."

"I still would have fallen in love with you," she insisted, kissing his fingers.

She could hear the smile in his voice. "I preferred not to take any chances—with that. And then I met Karen. Would you believe she's a distant relative of mine? It seems Abigail married a man from Charleston, so she must have recovered from Sam Calvert's death, after all. And Karen Striker is one of their descendants, which is how she got interested in the house. She came to work for me, and one day she came back from the costume shop with this dress—the one with the roses that you were wearing the day I found you in the garden. And that—'' he smiled ''—was when I knew it was going to happen. Destiny unfolding.''

Again the silence, the slow absorption of all the mysteries that went into the making of the great mystery of life. But something he had said about Karen caught in the back of Amelia's mind, disturbing her, and at last she moved a little away, looking at him.

''Jeff,'' she said uncertainly. ''Seven years. That's a long time. You must have met other women....''

His eyes twinkled. ''So I did. And all of them were just as fascinating as you said twentieth-century women would be. But...'' And the amusement left his eyes, to be replaced with gentle sobriety as he took her chin and held it steady between his fingers. ''None of them were you. And how could I care how fascinating any of them were when I was already married?''

She closed her eyes, lost in the swell of joy and certainty that was his kiss. It was true. He was here. She had come home.

Jeff brushed away the glimmer of a tear from her lashes and smiled. ''You said one time you could be happy running a place like this—setting the kind of table my mother used to set, making people feel welcome. Do you still think so?''

She could hardly draw a breath through the happiness that bubbled up inside her. ''I still have her recipes,'' she told him, and tapped her head. ''In here.''

"Good." The smile in his eyes deepened. "Because I sure could use a partner."

"Then you've got one."

"I have to tell you one thing, though," he warned, his expression growing serious. "There are a lot of things about this century I like, but the way people run around living together without the benefit of a preacher isn't one of them. I want it legal, and the sooner the better."

Amelia nodded. She couldn't stop smiling, and her voice was a little choked. "I think that can be arranged."

"Good." He caressed the back of her neck. "But in the meantime, I don't reckon there's any reason we couldn't have a little bit of the honeymoon first. I made reservations at the beach resort for us this weekend, if you want to go. I don't really think there's any reason for us to stay for this." He made a gesture toward the sound of voices and laughter from inside the house. "Do you?"

Amelia stood, holding his hands and bringing him with her. "No," she said, still smiling, still aching with joy. "I'll go get my things."

At the door she looked back and added, "After all, we already know how it ends."